THE
BILLIARD TABLE
MURDERS

THE BILLIARD TABLE MURDERS

A Gladys Babbington Morton Mystery

GLEN BAXTER

AVON BOOKS ◆ NEW YORK

AVON BOOKS
A division of
The Hearst Corporation
1350 Avenue of the Americas
New York, New York 10019

Copyright © 1990 by Glen Baxter
Back cover author photograph by Jo Agis
Published by arrangement with the author
Library of Congress Catalog Card Number: 91-92172
ISBN: 0-380-76668-X

First Avon Books Trade Printing: November 1991

AVON TRADEMARK REG. U.S. PAT. OFF. AND IN OTHER COUNTRIES, MARCA REGISTRADA, HECHO
EN U.S.A.

Printed in the U.S.A.

ARC   10 9 8 7 6 5 4 3 2 1

Gladys Babbington Morton is unhappy. Her first term at
St. Drunston's School is not without its problems. After one or two
minor explosions, there is an unpleasant surprise for Mr. Bradshaw
on the tennis courts. A flurry of staff unrest ensues, and Gladys is
enrolled at Crodlands, just off the Essex coast, where she is allowed
to pursue her interest in stump-work and research into toxic
chemicals. Unfortunately, Gladys becomes somewhat restless and
slips away to visit the ancestral home of the Babbington Mortons in
Scotland. It is not too long before she is relaxing on the croquet
lawns and beginning to think seriously about a career. The post of
cook at Morton Manor suddenly becomes vacant, and Roderick
Babbington Morton begins to suffer from a form of indigestion.
Gladys leaves for America, alighting in Manhattan just as Inspector
Trubcock arrives at Morton Manor.

FOR CAROLE

The author would like to thank Rudy Burckhardt, Ron Padgett &
Phyllis Zavatsky for their help during research on this book, and
Tientje for stepping in at the eleventh hour.
Especial thanks to Elisabeth and Jaco Groot for their invaluable
assistance during the Great Herring Crisis of March 1990.

Chapter One
AN UNEXPECTED GUEST

The Morton Manor, Scotland
Friday 14th June 1949, 10.55 a.m.

THE ANCIENT FAMILY SEAT OF
THE BABBINGTON MORTONS STOOD
PROUDLY ATOP THE HILLSIDE
OVERLOOKING THE TWEED VALLEY.
ALTHOUGH A NUMBER OF MINOR
EXTENSIONS HAD BEEN ADDED TO
THE MAIN BODY OF THE OLD HOUSE,
IT STILL MANAGED TO RETAIN
SOME OF THE CHARACTER OF A
TYPICAL EIGHTEENTH - CENTURY
SCOTTISH COUNTRY MANOR.

4

SHORTLY BEFORE 11 O'CLOCK
ON THE 14th JUNE 1949 A HOODED
FIGURE PASSED THROUGH THE
GATES AND HEADED SLOWLY
DOWN THE GRAVEL DRIVE.
    AT DAWN ON THE 15th THERE
CAME A SHARP KNOCK ON
THE DOOR.
  "MOST PEOPLE PREFER THE
BELL," ANNOUNCED THE BUTLER
AS HE SWUNG BACK THE
MASSIVE OAK DOOR.
  "WHOM SHALL I SAY IS CALLING?"

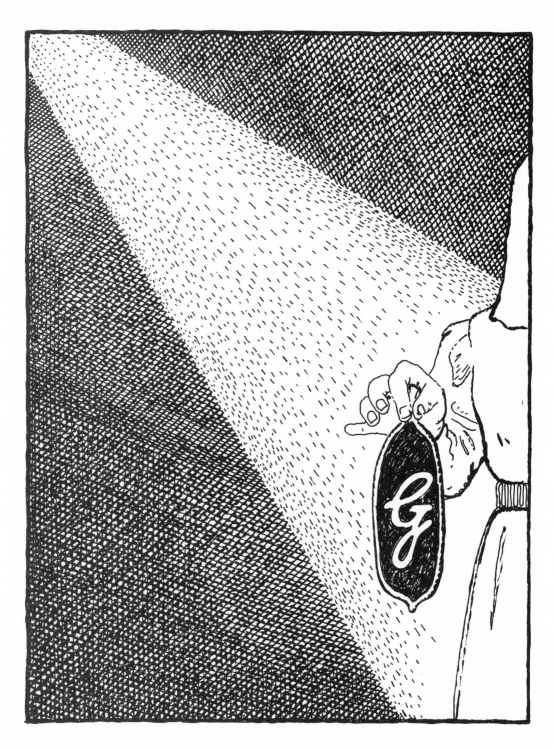

"JUST SHOW THIS TO MY UNCLE AND DON'T GET CUTE," SNAPPED THE HOODED ONE.

"VERY WELL, MADAM." THE
BUTLER TURNED ON HIS HEEL
AND DISAPPEARED INTO THE
GLOOM.

TWENTY MINUTES LATER,
RODERICK BABBINGTON MORTON
WAS STANDING IN THE HALLWAY,
EMBRACING HIS YOUNG NIECE.

"DEAR GLADYS, DO COME INTO
THE STUDY AND I'LL HAVE
SCRUTLEY SERVE TEA.

COME SIT BY THE FIRE AND
TELL ME ALL ABOUT THE
STRANGE HAPPENINGS AT
ST. DRUNSTON'S."

"YOU RECALL HOW I WROTE TO YOU ON MY FIRST DAY AT THE NEW SCHOOL? THINGS SEEMED TO GET OFF TO A BAD START. TINY, IRRITATING THINGS.

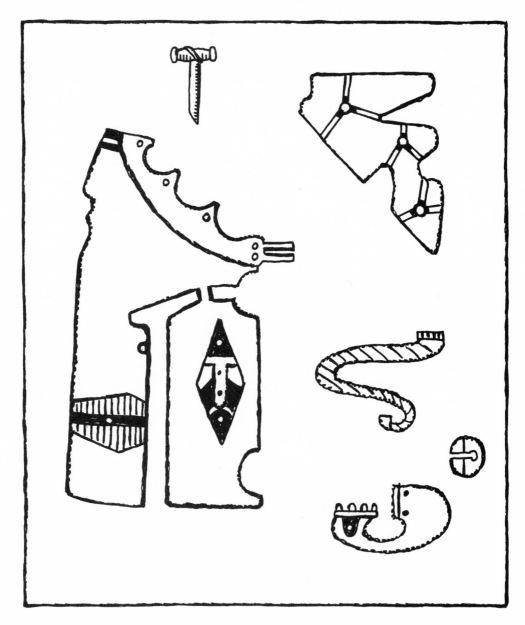

" I WAS NOT OVERLY IMPRESSED WITH THE SCHOOL UNIFORM.

"HOWEVER, I DECIDED TO
PUT ON A BRAVE FACE.

I WATCHED IN SILENCE
AS MY PARENTS PULLED OUT
OF THE DRIVE AND HEADED
BACK TO OUR LITTLE HOME
NESTLING IN THE COTSWOLDS.

I RAN MY FINGERS LIGHTLY
OVER THE NOTCHES IN MY
HOCKEY STICK AND
RESOLVED THERE AND THEN
TO MAKE SOMETHING OF
MYSELF AT ST. DRUNSTON'S.

"WELL, ON THE EVENING OF THE 3rd OF
OCTOBER, THE NEW CHEMISTRY LAB. WAS
DESTROYED BY A TREMENDOUS EXPLOSION.
FROM OUR DORMITORY WE COULD SEE THE
GLASS AND MOLTEN METAL RAINING
DOWN ON TO MR MURFITT'S
PRIZE MARROW BEDS.
IT WAS MOST
DISTRESSING.
MR. MURFITT
NEVER FULLY
RECOVERED.
I UNDERSTAND
HE WENT ON
TO PURSUE A
CAREER
IN POLITICS.

"IT SEEMED THAT ILL FORTUNE
DOGGED ST. DRUNSTON'S. MR. BRADSHAW,
WHO HAD BEEN ADVISED BY HIS DOCTOR
TO TAKE UP SPORT, WAS FOUND DEAD
ON THE TENNIS COURT JUST TWO WEEKS
LATER. HIS
OPPONENT, MISS
VERTLEY, WENT
ON TO WIN THREE
SETS TO LOVE
BEFORE SHE
REPORTED THE
TRAGEDY TO
MATRON, WHO
ARRIVED WITH
THE SCHOOL
WHEELBARROW.

"THERE WERE THOSE WHO EVEN
DARED TO SUGGEST THAT I HAD BEEN
INVOLVED IN THIS UNFORTUNATE
INCIDENT. SOME BUSYBODIES EVEN
WENT SO FAR AS TO SUGGEST THAT
I HAD CHOSEN MR BRADSHAW TO
PARTICIPATE IN MY EXPERIMENTAL
RESEARCH INTO CURARE AND ITS
MYRIAD USES. OF COURSE I DENIED
THIS. IT WAS TRUE THAT MY MAJOR
PROJECT FOR THAT TERM HAD BEEN
A STUDY OF THE FLORA AND FAUNA
OF SOUTH AMERICA AND I HAD BEEN
SIGHTED ON THE SCHOOL ROOF THAT
AFTERNOON. BUT I HAD MERELY
BEEN PRACTISING MY CLARINET...

"LIFE BECAME
INCREASINGLY DIFFICULT
FOR ME THERE.
  THE STAFF WERE OFTEN
UNSYMPATHETIC, SHORT-
TEMPERED AND OVERWEIGHT.
  EVEN MY FELLOW PUPILS
BEGAN TO OSTRACIZE ME.
  SO I PACKED MY KAZOO,
CLARINET AND TRIANGLE,
A SMALL SELECTION OF
BISCUITS, CAKES AND
CHISELS AND LEFT THE
DORMITORY.
  IT WAS NOT TOO LONG
BEFORE I FOUND
ALTERNATIVE
ACCOMMODATION.

15

"I'M AFRAID, THOUGH, THAT MY
DAYS AT ST. DRUNSTON'S WERE
DRAWING TO A CLOSE. ALICE
BARRACLOUGH, THE CLASS
SNEAK, SEARCHED MY DESK
WHILST I WAS STRUGGLING
WITH IMPORTANT RESEARCH
AT 'LE COQ D'OR' AND FOUND
THE PAPERS THAT LED TO MY
DISMISSAL..."

"BUT JUST WHAT WERE THESE
PAPERS, DEAR?" BUTTED IN
THE OLD MAN.

GLADYS PULLED OUT A SHEAF
OF NOTES AND LAID THEM
ON THE TABLE.

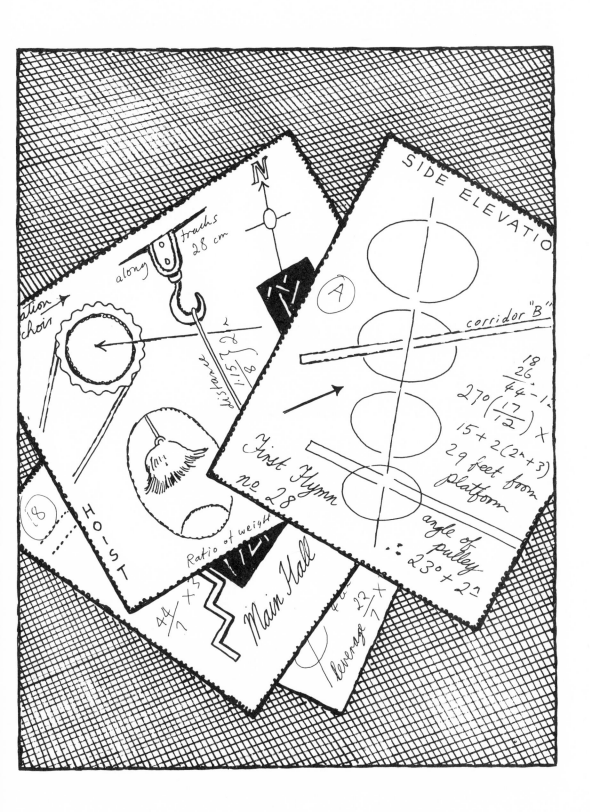

"THEY WERE CLAIMING THAT I HAD WORKED OUT AN ELABORATE SCHEME TO REMOVE THE CHOIRMASTER'S TOUPEE DURING THE FINAL BARS OF 'JERUSALEM'," SNORTED GLADYS INDIGNANTLY.

"I FAIL TO SEE HOW ANYONE COULD DEDUCE EVIDENCE OF CRIMINAL INTENT FROM THESE INNOCENT SKETCHES. NEEDLESS TO SAY, I HAD BEEN FRAMED."

"SO, HOW CAME YOU HERE?"

"WELL," CONTINUED GLADYS,
"THAT VERY SAME EVENING,
AN UNMARKED CAR DREW UP TO
THE BURSAR'S OFFICE. I WAS
BUNDLED INTO THE BACK AND
DRIVEN AT HIGH SPEED TO
MY NEXT SCHOOL..."

"WHICH WAS?" WHISPERED THE
OLD MAN.

"CRODLANDS, A SMALL
FORTIFIED ISLAND OFF THE
COAST OF ESSEX. IT WAS HERE
THAT I LEARNED TO WRITE
THREATENING LETTERS, FILL
OUT TAX RETURNS AND POLISH
UP MY STUMP WORK.

"OF COURSE, MY RESEARCH PROJECT ON SOUTH AMERICA CONTINUED, AS DID MY WORK ON CHEMICAL FORMULAE AND THE EXPERIMENTS WITH MATTER AND TIME."

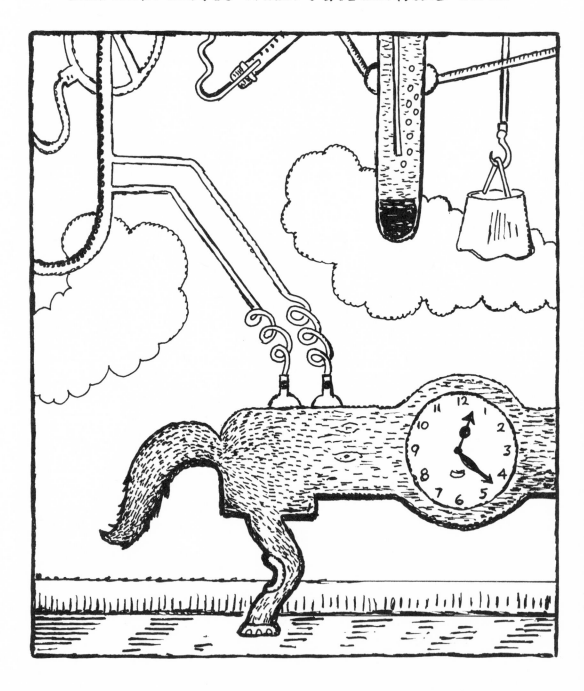

"BUT WHAT OF YOUR PARENTS?"
ENQUIRED UNCLE RODERICK.

"DON'T TALK TO ME ABOUT
THOSE TWO," HISSED GLADYS.
"THEY SOLD THE HOUSE, CHANGED
THEIR NAMES AND LEFT THE
COUNTRY WHEN I WROTE TO THEM
FOR A LITTLE EXTRA CASH TO
BUY SOME MUCH-NEEDED
CHEMICAL SUPPLIES."

"SO WHERE ARE THEY NOW?"

"NEEDLESS TO SAY, THEY LEFT
NO FORWARDING ADDRESS. BUT
I'LL FIND THEM, ONE FINE DAY.

"MY SCHOOLDAYS WERE DRAWING TO A CLOSE.
IT WAS TIME TO TAKE MY PLACE IN SOCIETY.

"I HAD A FEW QUIET WORDS WITH
THE STAFF AT CRODLANDS.

"AND I WAS GIVEN CARTE BLANCHE
TO LEAVE WHENEVER I CHOSE.

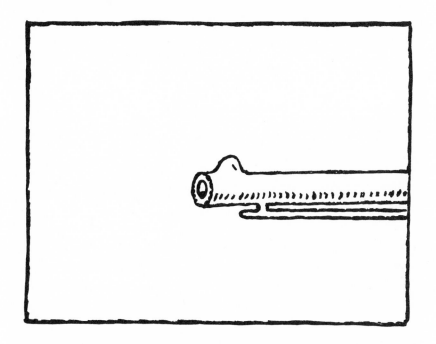

"SO, CHOKING BACK THE TEARS, I SAID
GOODBYE TO MY CHILDHOOD YEARS AND
SET OUT TO GREET THE GLORIOUS FUTURE."

"OH, GLADYS, YOU WERE ALWAYS SUCH A SCAMP,"
CHUCKLED UNCLE RODERICK. "WILL YOU STAY WITH
ME AWHILE? PERHAPS WE MIGHT DISCUSS THE
BABBINGTON MORTON FORTUNE. I KNOW OF YOUR
INTEREST IN MATTERS MATHEMATICAL AND FISCAL."

GLADYS BABBINGTON MORTON SLEPT SOUNDLY THAT
EVENING. THE NEXT MORNING SHE AWOKE AND TOOK
HER FIRST CIGAR OF THE DAY ON THE BALCONY OF
THE EAST WING, OVERLOOKING THE ROLLING HILLS.

"THERE'S NOTHING QUITE LIKE THE SCENT
OF FRESH HEATHER," SHE DRAWLED.

THE NEXT FEW WEEKS AT MORTON MANOR
PASSED SLOWLY . THESE WERE CAREFREE
DAYS SPENT PLAYING CROQUET, LOUNGING
ON THE TERRACE, POURING PORRIDGE INTO
THE RHODODENDRONS AND, IN THE EVENINGS,

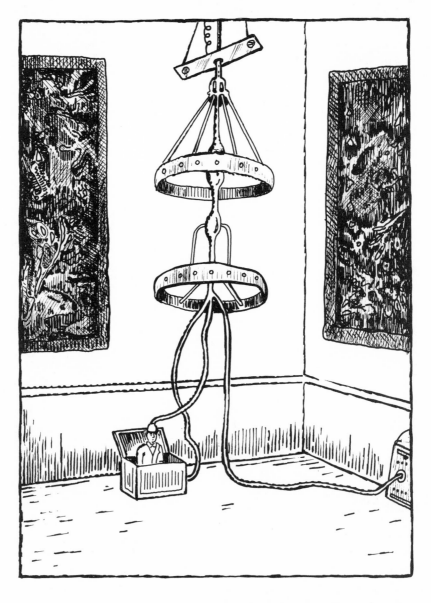

LISTENING TO THE FAMILY RADIO.

GRADUALLY, HOWEVER, EVEN THIS
IDYLLIC EXISTENCE BEGAN TO PALL.
GLADYS BECAME MOODY, DEPRESSED
AND IRRITABLE, OFTEN SPENDING
MANY HOURS ALONE IN THE POTTING
SHED. THINGS CAME TO A HEAD ONE
TUESDAY AFTERNOON WITH THE
INCIDENT ON THE CROQUET LAWN.
GLADYS THOUGHT
SHE HEARD MRS
PUTTOCK, THE COOK,
SNIGGER AS SHE
MISSED A
COMPARATIVELY
EASY SHOT

THROUGH A HOOP. SHE LOOKED UP
AND SAW THE BEECH HEDGE QUAKING.

THE TIME HAD CLEARLY COME TO
REMIND MRS PUTTOCK THAT AS A
SENSITIVE, CONTEMPLATIVE YOUNG GIRL

SHE DID NOT TAKE KINDLY TO ADVERSE
CRITICISM OF HER CROQUET TECHNIQUE.

DUE TO THE UNFORTUNATE ABSENCE
OF MRS. PUTTOCK THAT EVENING, GLADYS
TOOK OVER DUTIES IN THE KITCHEN,
TELLING THE KITCHEN STAFF, "THE
GREAT SECRET OF TUSCAN CUISINE IS
QUITE SIMPLE: ALWAYS USE THE FINEST
INGREDIENTS."

August 3rd

Porridge
— o —
Turnip purée á la McPherson
— o —
Cannelloni
— o —
Grilled parsnip in mead
— o —
Raspberries and cream served on a bed of porridge

HER UNCLE, SEATED AT THE LONG TABLE,
SCRUTINIZED THE MENU, SLOWLY SAVOURING
EACH IMPENDING CULINARY SPLENDOUR.

DR. Mc EWAN CYCLED UP FROM THE
VILLAGE THE NEXT MORNING TO
PRONOUNCE THE CAUSE OF DEATH
AS HEART FAILURE, YET EVEN AS
HE KNEELED BY THE BODY OF
RODERICK BABBINGTON MORTON HE
SENSED ALL WAS NOT WELL. STILL
CLUTCHED IN THE CORPSE'S HAND
WAS A LIGHTLY SCUFFED COPY
OF **"THE ART OF DIGGING"** BY
MORTIMER F. STUEDD.

A SUDDEN RUSTLING MADE HIM
TURN TO THE WINDOW.

HE RUSHED OUTSIDE. SOMETHING
WAS CLEARLY AMISS.

HIS SUSPICIONS WERE CONFIRMED
WHEN HE STUMBLED ON A FRAGMENT OF
CANNELLONI IN THE RHODODENDRONS.

HE RETURNED TO THE HOUSE,
TELEPHONED THE LOCAL POLICE
STATION AND MADE HIMSELF A
POT OF TEA. AN HOUR LATER,
CONSTABLE LEARKIN CYCLED UP
AND CORDONED OFF THE
RHODODENDRONS.

AN AMBULANCE ARRIVED AT
2.30 AND THE BODY WAS REMOVED
TO EDINBURGH CENTRAL FOR AN
AUTOPSY.

DR. Mc CUMMINGS TOOK OVER
AND SENT DOWN HIS REPORT TO
THE FORENSIC LABORATORY.

FOR TWO WEEKS A TEAM OF
EXPERTS PAINSTAKINGLY SIFTED
THROUGH THE EVIDENCE.

THEN, AT DAWN ON THE FIFTEENTH DAY, BENNINGER, HEAD OF FORENSIC, CYCLED OVER TO THE OFFICE OF CHIEF INSPECTOR MURDOCH. HE DARTED INTO THE ROOM AND ANNOUNCED:

"THE BOYS IN FORENSIC HAVE MANAGED TO RECONSTRUCT THE BABBINGTON MORTON MURDER WEAPON...

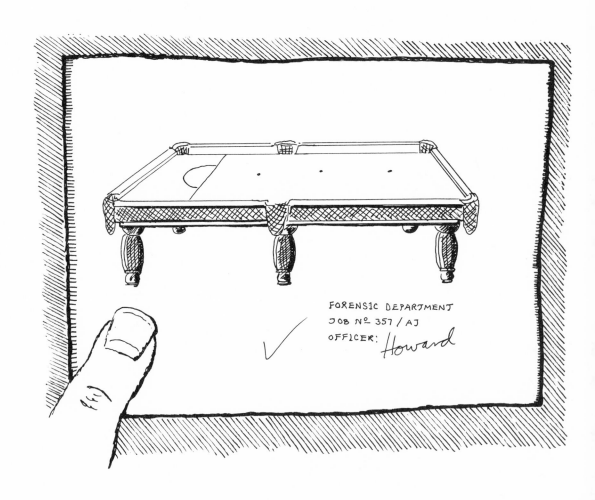

...HERE IT IS!"

MURDOCH'S FACE SANK. HE DROPPED
HIS BRAWN SANDWICH TO THE FLOOR.
"THIS IS MORE SERIOUS THAN I
THOUGHT," HE SAID GRAVELY. "WE'LL
HAVE TO CALL IN THE ONE MAN WHO
CAN HELP US NOW."

DETECTIVE INSPECTOR TRUBCOCK
REPLACED THE RECEIVER, LEFT
SCOTLAND YARD AND CAUGHT THE
NEXT TRAIN NORTH. AT EDINBURGH
STATION HE BOUGHT A NEWSPAPER.
THE HEADLINES WERE:

"DEATH BY BILLIARD TABLE"

Chapter Two
EMPIRE OF SPONGE

Switzerland Thursday
14th July 1949, 9.30 p.m.

SORGOR ARVIDSSON AWOKE EARLIER
THAN USUAL THAT GREY JULY EVENING.
STEPPING OVER THE MOUND OF SOILED
EPAULETTES, HE MADE HIS WAY OVER TO THE
WINDOW AND DREW BACK THE CURTAIN.

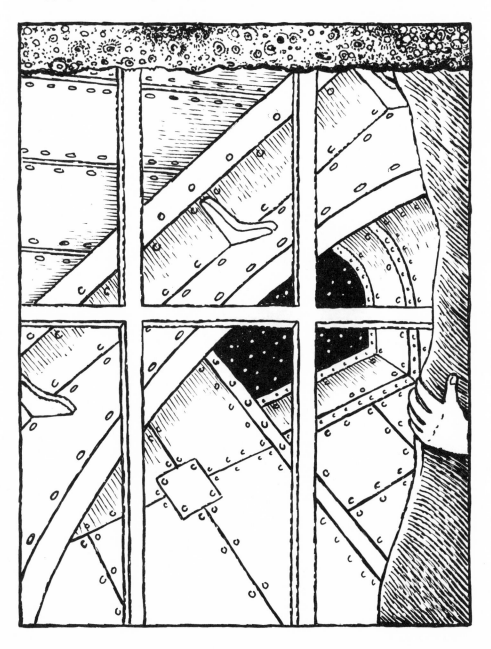

"MY BEAUTIFUL ZÜRICH!"
HE GROANED, REACHING
FOR THE ZINC-PLATED
CONE HE USED INSTEAD
OF BREAKFAST.
"I'M TIRED OF YOUR
PETTY OFFICIALS, THE
RANDOM EPAULETTE
INSPECTIONS AND
GENERAL DISDAIN FOR
MY WORKS.
"I WILL SEEK
RECOGNITION IN THE
NEW WORLD, SO FAREWELL!"

FOR SOME YEARS ARVIDSSON
HAD EKED OUT A MODEST LIVING
REPAIRING ZITHERS AND MAKING
FURNITURE. HIS WORK WAS
INSTANTLY RECOGNIZABLE, FOR,
ESCHEWING LOCAL MATERIALS,
HE HAD ELECTED TO WORK
EXCLUSIVELY IN SPONGE.

THINGS HAD NOT BEEN GOING
TOO WELL, HOWEVER. IN FACT, SINCE
1936 HE HAD RECEIVED ONLY TWO
COMMISSIONS, ONE FOR AN
ORNAMENTAL PIPE RACK AND, MORE
RECENTLY, ONE FOR A CUCKOO CLOCK.

HAVING COMPLETED THE CLOCK
IN RECORD TIME, HE WAS DEVASTATED
TO HEAR THAT HIS CLIENT HAD BEEN
ARRESTED IN A CHOCOLATE FACTORY,
CHARGED WITH INDUSTRIAL ESPIONAGE
AND SENT TO PRISON IN MADRID.

TOTALLY DISILLUSIONED, HE PACKED
HIS BAGS AND BOARDED THE NIGHT
TRAIN TO MARSEILLES.

FROM HERE HE WOULD SAIL TO AMERICA
AND START A NEW LIFE, HIS VISION OF A
VAST SPONGE EMPIRE AS YET UNDIMMED.

BY DAY HE SAT ALONE IN HIS TINY CABIN
WORKING ON NEW DESIGNS. BY NIGHT HIS
HEART BEGAN TO BEAT TO A DIFFERENT
DRUM, AND HE WOULD ENTERTAIN THOSE
DINING IN FIRST CLASS WITH AN EXHIBITION
OF VIRTUOSO SPONGE-TAP ROUTINES TO THE
MUSIC OF RODGERS & HAMMERSTEIN.

"HE MAY NOT BE THE GREATEST TAPDANCER
I'VE EVER SEEN," REMARKED FELLOW
PASSENGER OGDEN LOMAX JNR. "BUT HE
SURE IS THE QUIETEST."
    AS THE LINER DOCKED IN MANHATTAN,
ARVIDSSON STOOD ON DECK, BLOWING A
FANFARE ON HIS SPONGE BUGLE.

Chapter Three
A HASTY DEPARTURE

The Croquet Lawn, Morton Mano.
Midnight, 24ᵗʰ August 1949

"WE REALLY NEED TO SPEAK TO HIS NIECE, GLADYS," NOTED DETECTIVE INSPECTOR TRUBCOCK, AS HIS WEATHERBEATEN HANDS MOVED SLOWLY DOWN THE CHIPPED SHAFT OF THE CROQUET MALLET HE HAD FOUND TUCKED BEHIND THE TEN VOLUMES OF "**BATTERY OPERATED LAMPS AND THEIR USAGE AFLOAT**" BY A. R. GOURGE IN THE LIBRARY OF MORTON MANOR. "I'M AFRAID THERE'S STILL NO SIGN OF HER," REPLIED CONSTABLE LEARKIN.

"I'D LIKE TO KNOW WHERE SHE IS RIGHT NOW," MUTTERED TRUBCOCK.

GLADYS WAS ABOUT TO BID
FAREWELL TO SCOTLAND

AND HEAD OUT TOWARDS
THE SETTING SUN.

WEEKS LATER, SHE AWOKE TO SEE THE
SKYLINE OF MANHATTAN.

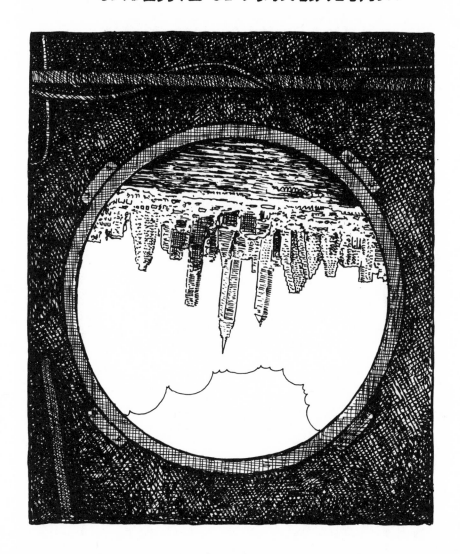

BEING A STOWAWAY ABOARD A VENEZUELAN
FREIGHTER WAS NOT WITHOUT ITS DRAWBACKS,
OF WHICH SLEEPING HANGING FROM A TRAPEZE
IN THE BROOM CLOSET WAS BUT ONE. NOBODY
ON PIER 86 NOTICED THE HOODED FIGURE SLIP
ASHORE TO VANISH INTO THE NEW YORK NIGHT.

45

Chapter Four

MISS HARRINGTON
SPEAKS OUT

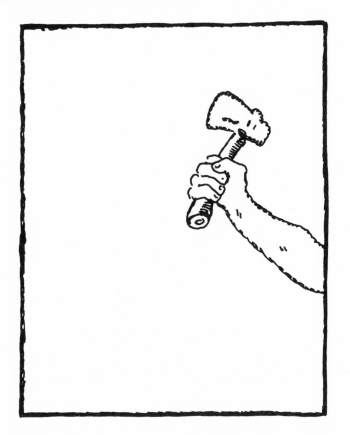

St. Drunston's School, Sussex
Tuesday 8th September
1949, 2.45 p.m.

INSPECTOR TRUBCOCK WOUND DOWN THE
WINDOW OF THE BLACK ROVER SALOON
AND PEERED OUT AT THE TOWERS OF
ST. DRUNSTON'S UPPER SCHOOL. A SHORT
TIME LATER HE WAS SEATED IN THE STUDY
OF MISS BEATRICE HARRINGTON.

HEADMISTRESS

"WELL, YOU KNOW, DEAR GLADYS WAS AN EXTRAORDINARY GIRL. GIFTED ACADEMICALLY ALTHOUGH OFTEN UNPOPULAR WITH HER PEERS, AS IS OFTEN THE CASE WITH EXCEPTIONAL STUDENTS. HER ESSAY 'HIDDEN SYMBOLISM IN THE WORK OF VITTORE CARPACCIO, WITH SPECIAL REFERENCE TO THE VISION OF ST. AUGUSTINE' BROUGHT TEARS TO THE EYES OF MISS PLANGBOURNE, THE EXTERNAL EXAMINER, BUT ONLY GROANS FROM HER FELLOW STUDENTS, AND I DARE SAY MORE THAN A LITTLE RESENTMENT."

"I MUST ADMIT, THOUGH, THAT MY
SUSPICIONS WERE FIRST ROUSED
WHEN SHE PROPOSED A CHANGE OF
OUTFIT FOR THE THIRD-YEAR
HOCKEY TEAM FOR AWAY GAMES.

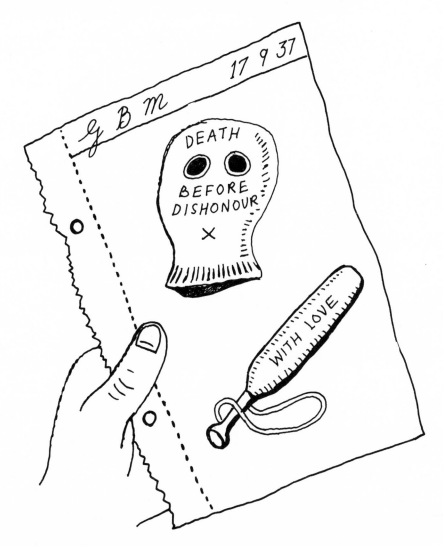

"THIS IS THE SKETCH SHE HANDED IN
AT THE TIME. I HAD A FEELING IT MIGHT
TURN OUT TO BE IMPORTANT ONE DAY.

"NATURALLY, WE CONTINUED WITH
THE EXISTING UNIFORM AND THAT
WAS THE LAST WE HEARD OF IT.
   GLADYS REFUSED TO DISCUSS THE
INCIDENT, AND INDEED DENIED THAT
IT HAD EVER TAKEN PLACE."
   "BUT WHAT ABOUT THE TENNIS-
COURT DEATH AND THE MORE SERIOUS
ALLEGATION THAT GLADYS WAS THE
BRAINS BEHIND THE PLOT TO
HUMILIATE THE CHOIRMASTER ON
SPEECH DAY?" ENQUIRED TRUBCOCK.
   "IT WAS INDEED A VERY DIFFICULT
TIME FOR THE SCHOOL," NOTED THE
HEADMISTRESS.

"SCHOOL MEALS WERE CANCELLED

AND SECURITY WAS STEPPED UP."

"AND IS IT NOT ALSO TRUE THAT
GLADYS WAS REMOVED FROM SCHOOL
AFTER DARK AND HER PAPERS
MYSTERIOUSLY MISLAID, AND THAT,
FURTHERMORE, A CELEBRATION
DINNER WAS HELD IN THE SENIOR
COMMON ROOM AT WHICH A TOTAL OF
**TWO HUNDRED AND SIXTY-THREE
OF CHÂTEAU LAFITTE '28** WERE
CONSUMED?" BARKED TRUBCOCK.

"WE WERE ALL COMPLETELY
DEVASTATED," REPLIED THE HEAD-
MISTRESS.

"THANK YOU, MISS HARRINGTON. THAT
WILL BE ALL FOR NOW", REMARKED
THE DETECTIVE AS HE OPENED THE
WINDOW TO LEAVE.

Chapter Five
A FATEFUL CALL

Ratner's Restaurant, Second Avenue,
New York City Monday 8th October
1949, 7.35 p.m.

GLADYS HAD TAKEN UP RESIDENCE
AT 342 EAST THIRTEENTH STREET.
HAVING SIGNED THE TENANCY
AGREEMENT DAPHNE BRACEGIRDLE,
OCCUPATION "GOVERNESS."

SHE REALLY LIKED NEW YORK,
ALTHOUGH SHE WAS HAVING SOME
PROBLEMS WITH AMERICAN FOOD.
EACH EVENING SAW HER STRUGGLING
WITH THE COMPLEXITIES OF THE
LOCAL MENUS.

GRADUALLY HER FUNDS BEGAN TO DWINDLE AND GLADYS TOOK TO SCANNING THE "SITUATIONS VACANT" COLUMNS INSTEAD OF MENUS.

THUS IT WAS ON THAT FATEFUL DAY OF 16th APRIL 1951 THAT GLADYS MADE THE TELEPHONE CALL THAT WAS TO CHANGE THE LIVES OF THE OCCUPANTS OF 263 EAST EIGHTY-NINTH STREET.

"I AM ENQUIRING ABOUT THE POST OF HOUSEKEEPER TO MR. AND MRS. GEFFEN. MY NAME IS DAPHNE BRACEGIRDLE AND MY CREDENTIALS ARE IMPECCABLE."

ON THE 6th OF MAY, THE HEADLINES OF THE NEW YORK POST READ:

"WEALTHY LAWYER AND WIFE FOUND DEAD ON UPPER EAST SIDE."

THEN, TWO DAYS LATER, THE SAME
NEWSPAPER CARRIED THE HEADLINE:
"MYSTERY POISON IN GEFFEN
CASE BAFFLES EXPERTS."
GLADYS TURNED THE PAGE, RAN HER
FINGER DOWN THE "SITUATIONS
VACANT" COLUMNS AND STOPPED AT
AN ADDRESS ON SUTTON PLACE. SHE
DIALLED THE NUMBER PRINTED
THERE AND SAID SOFTLY,
"GOOD MORNING. MY NAME IS LUCY
BUFFINGTON, OF WINDSOR, ENGLAND,
AND I'M CALLING ABOUT THE POST OF
ASSISTANT TO MR. GRANTHE."
"HOLD THE LINE, PLEAT..."
ANSWERED A STRANGELY HIGH-
PITCHED VOICE.

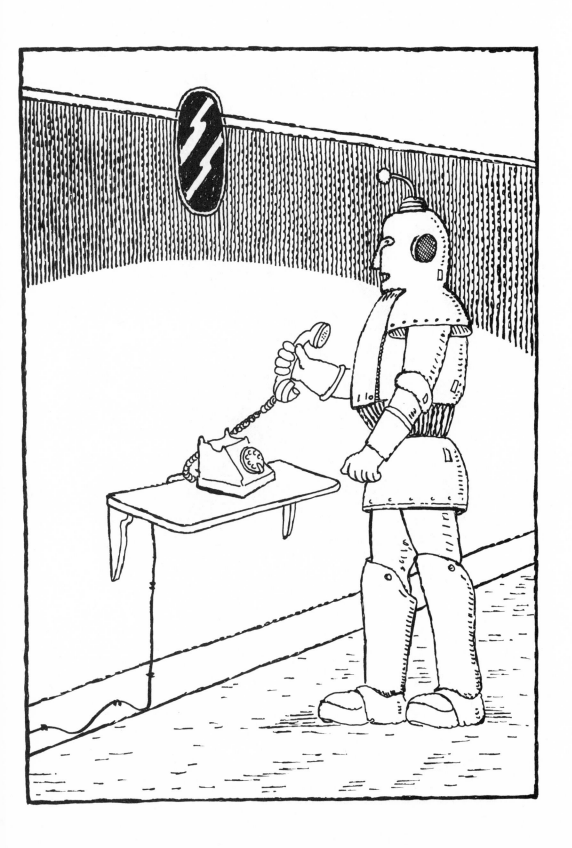

57

LESS THAN AN HOUR LATER, THE ROBOT, KNOWN AFFECTIONATELY AS McNALLY, USHERED GLADYS INTO THE DRAWING ROOM OF THE GRANTHE MANSION ON

SUTTON PLACE. OUT OF THE DARKNESS STEPPED HER NEW EMPLOYER, TYLER GRANTHE.

"WELCOME, MISS BUFFINGTON, TO MY WORLD," HE ANNOUNCED.

"YOU SEE, I AM AN INVENTOR.
AT PRESENT I AM WORKING ON A
SYSTEM TO INCORPORATE A
GRAMOPHONE INTO THE HAT ALSO.
YOUR POSITION HERE WILL BE TO
FILE MY INVENTIONS EACH DAY AT
THE PATENT OFFICE. McNALLY WILL
ASSIST."

"WHEN DO I BEGIN?"

"THERE'S NO TIME LIKE THE
PRESENT, ESPECIALLY FOR WEARERS
OF THE GRANTHE CHRONOMETER,
US PATENT PENDING, IS THERE,
McNALLY?"

"TEMPIS FUGIT," SQUEAKED BACK
THE ROBOT.

Chapter Six

QUESTIONS AND ANSWERS

Room 236, Scotland Yard,
London Wednesday 2nd April
1951, 9.15 a.m.

"I'VE FOUND HER, INSPECTOR!"
EXCLAIMED SERGEANT BLOSTOVER.
"DIANA Mc CURDY, FORTY-THREE
MARINE AVENUE, HOVE, EAST SUSSEX."
HE PLACED THE TELEPHONE
DIRECTORY ON TRUBCOCK'S DESK.
"EXCELLENT! GET THE CAR!"
ANNOUNCED TRUBCOCK.

THE WHEELS OF THE ROVER ROLLED
TO A HALT IN MARINE AVENUE.
TRUBCOCK SWITCHED OFF THE
ENGINE, GOT OUT AND RANG THE
DOORBELL OF NUMBER 43.
"I SUPPOSE YOU'VE CALLED ABOUT
GLADYS?"DRAWLED DIANA Mc CURDY.
"YOU'D BETTER COME INSIDE."

"YOU NOTICED MY SCAR?"

TRUBCOCK LOOKED DOWN AT THE CARPET. THE DESIGN WAS ALMOST PLEASANT.

"YES, IT'S TRUE GLADYS AND I DID NOT ALWAYS SEE EYE TO EYE, ESPECIALLY OVER THE SIMPSON AFFAIR."

"JANET STIMPSON?" ENQUIRED TRUBCOCK.

"NO, JANET SIMPSON," REPLIED Mc CURDY.

"THE UNFORTUNATE GIRL WHO BORROWED A PENCIL FROM GLADYS AND FORGET TO RETURN IT."

"AND...?" INTERRUPTED TRUBCOCK.

"WELL, I SUGGESTED SOME MINOR PUNISHMENT, SUCH AS A THIRTY-MINUTE BARRAGE OF PUNNING, BUT GLADYS THOUGHT OTHERWISE.

"THEY FOUND JANET'S NUMBER THREE
IRON ON THE SEVENTEENTH GREEN THE
FOLLOWING DAY.

"IT SEEMED ODD, AS SHE USUALLY TOOK
A WOOD ON THE SEVENTEENTH..."

"WAS THERE NOT AN INVESTIGATION?"
"OF COURSE, BUT AS EVER IT PROVED
INCONCLUSIVE," ADDED McCURDY.
  "BUT WERE YOU YOURSELF NOT AFRAID
AFTER THAT?"
  "ONLY IN THE EVENINGS. I SIMPLY
CHANGED MY SLEEPING HABITS."

Chapter Seven
TRYING TIMES

Hell's Kitchen, Manhattan
Friday 19th April 1951, 1.06 p.m.

EDWIN SCHUYLER CLOSED THE DOOR OF
HIS OPTICIAN'S SHOP AND STEPPED OUT
INTO THE BUSTLE OF NINTH AVENUE.
  HE WALKED UP TO MANGANARO'S
DELICATESSEN AND NOTICED A FIGURE
PEERING IN THE WINDOW THERE.
  "TOGO!" CALLED OUT THE OPTICIAN.
  THE FIGURE TURNED ROUND.
  "YOU BUY CUCKOO CLOCK?" BEAMED
SORGOR ARVIDSSON.
  "SORRY. MY MISTAKE," BUMBLED
SCHUYLER, AND BUSTLED ON UP TO
THIRTY-NINTH STREET.
  SORGOR ARVIDSSON WAS HAVING
PROBLEMS. THE MARKET FOR SPONGE-
WARE IN NEW YORK WAS REMARKABLY
THIN. HE LOOKED UP.

HIS SATURATION ADVERTISING CAMPAIGN WAS
STILL NOT PRODUCING A CONSUMER STAMPEDE.

Chapter Eight
STRANGE ENCOUNTERS

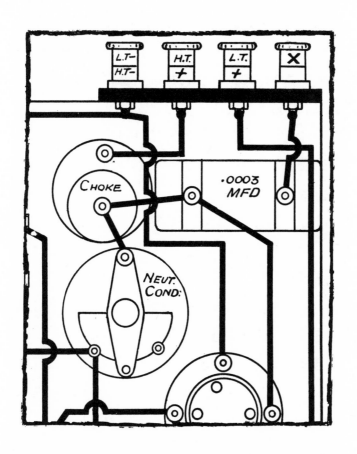

Sutton Place, Manhattan
Tuesday 14th June 1951, 8.30 p.m.

THE DINNER GONG SOUNDED.
MᶜNALLY ENTERED THE DINING
ROOM AND ANNOUNCED,
  "GINNER ISH DERVED!"
  GLADYS TOOK THE LIFT DOWN TO
THE THIRD FLOOR AND ENTERED
THE ROOM.
  "MISS BUFFINGTON, I'D LIKE TO
INTRODUCE MY WIFE, REBECCA,"
WHISPERED MR. GRANTHE.
  "CHARMED I'M SURE", NOTED GLADYS
AS SHE CROSSED THE ROOM,
DISCREETLY STUBBED OUT HER
CIGAR IN THE FRUIT BOWL AND
SAT DOWN AT THE TABLE.
  "LET'S EAT!"

DURING DINNER THE THREE OF THEM
DISCUSSED THE WORLD OF ART, BASE-
BALL AND THE EVER-INCREASING
DEMAND FOR EUCALYPTUS LEAVES.

MC NALLY BROUGHT IN THE DESSERT.
"SHORE-BAY," HE CROAKED.

"FORGIVE ME, LADIES. THERE IS STILL
MUCH WORK TO BE DONE ON MC NALLY,"
ANNOUNCED MR. GRANTHE, REACHING
FOR HIS NAPKIN.

THE WEEKS PASSED BY AND ONCE AGAIN
GLADYS BEGAN TO FEEL RESTLESS,
SPENDING MUCH OF HER SPARE TIME
ALONE IN HER ROOM, TOYING WITH
HER CROSSBOW.

IT WAS NOT TOO LONG BEFORE SHE TOOK
TO SLIPPING OUT AT NIGHTS AND
HEADING DOWNTOWN.

ONE EVENING, IN A BAR ON EAST
TWELFTH STREET, SHE WAS
APPROACHED BY A STRANGE YOUNG MAN.
"YOU MIGHT BE INTERESTED IN MY
CARD," HE WHISPERED.

"WHY, IT'S A RECTANGLE!" CRIED GLADYS.
"YOU ENGLISH OR SOMETHING?" RASPED
THE STRANGER.
"TRY THE OTHER SIDE, DUMBO..."

Eugene Lundy
EXTORTION: LOAN SHARKING MAYHEM TO ORDER: HOUSES CLEARED ETC.
Tel 589 4263

"BEEN IN THE BUSINESS LONG?" QUIPPED GLADYS.

"LONG ENOUGH", REPLIED MR. LUNDY, CASUALLY FINGERING A SILVER, MOTHER-OF-PEARL AND EMERALD KNUCKLEDUSTER.

IT WAS THE BEGINNING OF A WHIRLWIND ROMANCE.

GLADYS BEGAN SEEING MORE AND MORE OF EUGENE, HER FIRST LOVE. THINGS WERE PROCEEDING EXCEPTIONALLY WELL UNTIL THE 14th OF AUGUST, WHEN SHE ARRANGED TO MEET HIM AFTER WORK.

THAT EVENING, BACK AT HIS APARTMENT
ON THE UPPER EAST SIDE

EVENTS BEGAN TO TAKE A SINISTER TURN...

IT WAS A LITTLE INDISCRETION THAT
WAS TO COST EUGENE DEAR. FOUR NIGHTS
LATER, GLADYS COOKED HIS DINNER.

GLADYS OPENED THE NEW YORK HERALD AND
READ:"SMALL TIME HOODLUM, EUGENE LUNDI
A.K.A JACK 'BOBO' TRUNKLE, WAS FOUND DEAD
IN HIS APARTMENT ON E. 83rd ST."

SHE RETURNED TO WORK THE NEXT
DAY TO FIND MR. GRANTHE ABSORBED
IN HIS LATEST PROJECT, № 4256 JS/21A.

THE ANTI-KIDNAP DECOY ATTACHMENT

"I'D LIKE YOU TO POP THESE PAPERS DOWN TO
THE PATENT OFFICE, MY DEAR," HE BEAMED.

A CHANCE MEETING WITH A YOUNG HOCKEY
PLAYER IN THE LOBBY OF THE PATENT
OFFICE LED TO ANOTHER ROMANCE WHICH
UNFORTUNATELY ENDED RATHER ABRUPTLY
ONE EVENING AT HIS APARTMENT ON
GREENWICH AVENUE.

"SMELLS GOOD, LUCY. IS THIS YOUR SPECIALITY?"

GLADYS SEEMED TO BE EXPERIENCING
A LITTLE TROUBLE WITH AMERICAN
MEN, AS A GLANCE AT THE ORBITUARY
COLUMNS WOULD TESTIFY.

IT WAS ON 19th AUGUST OF THAT YEAR
THAT THE SENSATIONAL LINK IN THE
RECENT POISONINGS WAS ANNOUNCED.

FORENSIC EXPERTS AT THE
TENTH PRECINCT PLACED A SHEAF
OF DOCUMENTS ON DETECTIVE
INSPECTOR MULHEARDY'S DESK.
HE SWIVELLED ROUND IN HIS CHAIR
AND READ ALOUD FROM THE
MORNING NEWSPAPER:
"DISTURBING NEW EVIDENCE
POINTS CONCLUSIVELY TO BIZARRE
CONNECTION IN RECENT HOMICIDES.
VICTIMS ALL SLAIN BY BILLIARD
TABLES."
HE LOWERED HIS EYES. "THIS IS ALL
WE NEED."

Chapter Nine
ROMANCE IN THE AIR

Waverly Place, Manhattan
Thursday 15th September 1951, 7.28 p.m.

GLADYS WAS NOW FIRMLY ESTABLISHED ON THE SOCIAL SCENE. EVERYBODY WANTED TO MEET LUCY BUFFINGTON, THE CHARMING ENGLISH GIRL.

"ALLOW ME TO INTRODUCE MYSELF—THEODORE BAHNWEILER," ANNOUNCED ONE SUCH ADMIRER AT A COCKTAIL PARTY IN GREENWICH VILLAGE.

"ONE DAY THE WHOLE WORLD WILL COME TO KNOW MY NAME AND THAT OF YOURS TOO, PERHAPS."

"HOW SO?" ENQUIRED GLADYS.

"I INTEND TO REWRITE THE HISTORY OF THE AIRSHIP AND REMOVE THE SHADOW OF THE HINDENBURG FOR EVER."

"JOLLY INTERESTING," NOTED GLADYS AS SHE SLIPPED AWAY INTO THE KITCHEN.

THE NEXT MORNING, AS GLADYS WAS
STROLLING THROUGH CENTRAL PARK,
A PINK CARD LANDED AT HER FEET.

Dear Miss Buffington,
 You are looking
at the future. Together
we can conquer the
world. Please meet
me on Tuesday at
12.30, corner of 42nd
and Madison to discover
your true destiny
 yours,
 Theodore Bahnweiler

GLADYS LOOKED UP.

ACCORDINGLY, ON TUESDAY AT THE
APPOINTED HOUR, GLADYS MET MR.
BAHNWEILER AND WAS WHISKED BY
LIMOUSINE OUT TO LAKEHURST, NJ,
WHERE SHE WAS TO RECEIVE A
SOMEWHAT UNUSUAL ENGAGEMENT
PRESENT.

FROM THAT MOMENT ON, GLADYS
WOULD SPEND HER WEEKENDS MASTERING
THE CONTROLS OF THE MIGHTY CRAFT.

Chapter Ten

ENTER TRUBCOCK AND MULHEARDY

"The Beeches", Lower Biddlington, Kent 29th August 1951, Teatime

"ANOTHER SCONE, DEAR?"
QUERIED MRS. EDNA TRUBCOCK.

"NO THANK YOU, DEAR," GROANED HER
HUSBAND. "THERE'S SOMETHING HERE
IN THE TIMES ABOUT A BIZARRE
MURDER IN NEW YORK, ONE OF THE MOST
BAFFLING CASES EVER TO COME BEFORE
OUR COLLEAGUES IN THAT PECULIAR CITY.

I HAVE A FEELING THAT THERE IS
A CONNECTION WITH THE LITTLE
UNPLEASANTNESS IN SCOTLAND."

"WILL YOU BE TAKING THAT SCONE NOW,
DEAR?"

"NO, I THINK I'LL BE APPLYING FOR THE
NECESSARY PAPERS TO GO OUT THERE
AND CHECK THE DETAILS AGAINST MY
FILE ON MISS BABBINGTON MORTON."

"MORE TEA, DEAR?"

"NO, I MUST LEAVE FOR SCOTLAND YARD
IMMEDIATELY. THERE'S NO TIME TO LOSE!"

EXACTLY TEN DAYS LATER, THE DETECTIVE
INSPECTOR BOARDED THE STEAMER
"SS ORLANDO" BOUND FOR NEW YORK.

AS THE STEAMER ENTERED THE VERRAZANO NARROWS, TRUBCOCK SCRIBBLED IN HIS NOTEPAD...

...UNAWARE THAT HIS ARRIVAL IN THE NEW WORLD WAS NOT PASSING UNNOTICED.

THE VERY FIRST THING HE DID WAS TAKE A TAXI ACROSS TOWN TO THE TENTH PRECINCT OFFICE WHERE HIS AMERICAN COUNTERPART, DETECTIVE INSPECTOR LAWRENCE MULHEARDY OF HOMICIDE, WAS AWAITING HIS ARRIVAL.

NO SOONER HAD THEY MET THAN A CALL CAME THROUGH.

"SUSPECTED HOMICIDE AT NINETEEN WEST TWENTY-SECOND STREET."

TRUBCOCK AND MULHEARDY RACED TO THE SCENE.

IT WAS TRUBCOCK WHO FIRST
NOTICED THE HALF-EATEN BOWL
OF PASTA ON THE TABLE.

THE VICTIM'S INDEX FINGER BORE
TRACES OF A GREENISH SAUCE AND THERE,
ON THE CARPET, HE HAD WRITTEN:

Joseph Thum
1241 Broadway

"WHAT'S THAT?" QUERIED MULHEARDY.
"USED TO BE A BILLIARD SALON, AS FAR AS I
KNOW, OLD CHAP," REPLIED TRUBCOCK.
   A COOL BREEZE WAS BLOWING THROUGH
THE ROOM. MULHEARDY STEPPED INTO
THE KITCHEN, NOTICED THE OPEN WINDOW
AND LEANED OUT.
   "OVER THERE, QUICK!" HE YELLED.

"THESE MARKS ARE ENTIRELY
CONSISTENT WITH A BILLIARD TABLE
BEING DRAGGED THROUGH HERE."

"JUST WHAT IS ALL THIS MALARKY WITH THE BILLIARD TABLES, TRUBCOCK?" SNORTED MULHEARDY.

"WELL, IT SEEMS THAT SEPARATELY ALL THE ELEMENTS OF A BILLIARD TABLE — THE GREEN BAIZE CLOTH, WOOD, SLATE AND BRASS FITTINGS — ARE PERFECTLY SAFE IN THEMSELVES, BUT WHEN MIXED TOGETHER A PECULIAR CHEMICAL REACTION TAKES PLACE. IT'S SOMETHING TO DO WITH THE ACID LEVELS IN THE GROUND SLATE SETTING OFF A CHAIN REACTION WITH THE MINUTE QUANTITY OF ARSENIC IN THE BAIZE, BRASS AND WOOD. THE RESULTING COMPOUND IS UTTERLY DEADLY."

"BUT WHAT OF THE RUBBER CUSHIONS
AND THE POCKETS?" ASKED MULHEARDY.

"THEY MERELY SERVE AS A STABILIZING
FORCE DURING THE REACTION," ADDED TRUBCOCK.

Chapter Eleven
THE MASKED BALL

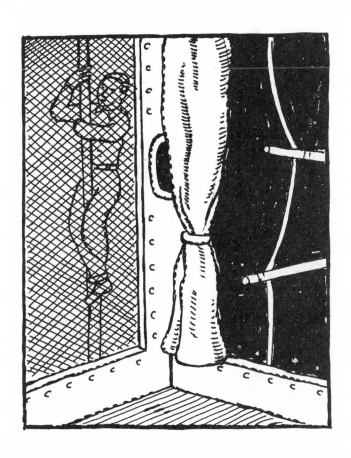

Sutton Place, Manhattan
1st October 1951, 11.45 p.m.

GLADYS MINGLED WITH THE OTHER
GUESTS IN THE LOUNGE.

WHERE SHE WAS INTRODUCED TO
GOREM BREISSEL, THE SURREALIST
SCULPTOR FROM CARDIFF, WHOSE
CONCRETE AND LEATHER "CLOUD WORKS"
WERE THE TALK OF GREENWICH VILLAGE.
  THEN GLADYS WAS MOVED ALONG TO
MEET RANDOLPH PRESCOTT JNR, ONE
OF MANHATTAN'S LEADING COLLECTORS
OF MODERN ART.
  "MISS BUFFINGTON, I AM CHARMED,"
HE ANNOUNCED.
  "AH, MR. PRESCOTT, WHAT IS YOUR
FAVOURITE PIECE OF THOSE YOU'VE
COLLECTED?" ENQUIRED GLADYS.
  "WITHOUT DOUBT, THE JEWEL OF
MY DUTCH MASTERS COLLECTION
IS THE VERY RARE PIECE, THE
RIETVELD BIDET."

"BUT DO TELL ME ABOUT ERIC BLOHST, THE PROLIFIC YOUNG PAINTER WHO HAS TAKEN THE ART WORLD BY STORM," DEMANDED GLADYS.

"YOUNG ERIC, YES. I WAS FORTUNATE ENOUGH TO VISIT HIS STUDIO AND OBSERVE HIS REMARKABLE TECHNIQUE," REPLIED THE COLLECTOR. "MISS BUFFINGTON? ASKED A FAMILIAR VOICE. GLADYS TURNED AND CAME FACE TO FACE WITH HER EMPLOYER.

"LUCY, MY DEAR, THERE IS SOMETHING
I HAVE TO TELL YOU."

Chapter Twelve

TRUBCOCK EXPLAINS

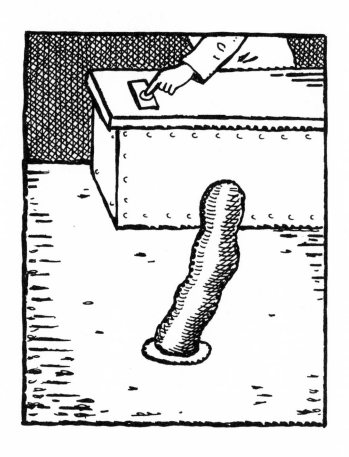

N.Y.P.D. 10th Precinct, Manhattan
4th October 1951, 10.25 a.m.

DETECTIVE MULHEARDY STUBBED OUT HIS CIGARETTE IN THE ASHTRAY AND WATCHED THE BLUE SMOKE CURL SLOWLY UPWARDS TO MEET THE GAZE OF HIS ENGLISH COLLEAGUE.

"WELL, I THINK WE MAY BE GETTING SOMEWHERE. I'VE HAD AN AGENT STAKING OUT HESTER STREET FOR THE PAST THREE DAYS.

"AND WE'VE JUST RECIEVED A TIP-OFF
THAT OUR PRIME SUSPECT LIVES ON EAST
TWELFTH STREET BETWEEN FIRST AVENUE
AND AVENUE A. I'VE SENT MOCHALSKI
AND LENHART OVER TO CHECK IT OUT.
THEY SHOULD BE THERE ABOUT NOW."

"JUST WHAT KIND OF WOMAN
ARE WE UP AGAINST?"
ENQUIRED MULHEARDY.

"WELL, WHEN SHE WAS
FOURTEEN, SHE MADE CERTAIN
THAT SHE CARRIED OFF THE
ST. DRUNSTON'S TENNIS CUP,"
REPLIED TRUBCOCK.

"NOTHING WRONG IN THAT,"
BUTTED IN MULHEARDY.

"NO. EXCEPT THAT THERE
WERE THOSE WHO SWEAR
THAT HER OPPONENT'S
RACKET HAD BEEN
TAMPERED WITH."

107

"AND THE OUTCOME OF THE
GAME?"

"GLADYS WAS LEADING
FIVE-FOUR WHEN HER
OPPONENT LUCY MATHER
EXPLODED."

"EXPLODED?" GASPED
MULHEARDY.

"YES, AT THE TIME IT WAS
THOUGHT TO BE ONE OF
ENGLAND'S MOST
EXTRAORDINARY CASES OF
SPONTANEOUS COMBUSTION.
BUT LOOKING BACK NOW,
I'M NOT SO SURE..."

"ARE YOU SUGGESTING THAT IT WAS NOT AN ISOLATED INCIDENT?"

"I'M AFRAID SO," RESPONDED TRUBCOCK. "THE TROUBLE WITH OUR MISS MORTON GOES WAY BACK.

"BEFORE I LEFT ENGLAND I PAID A VISIT TO HER OLD NURSERY SHOOL IN LOWER CHEADLEY. THE STAFF THERE SHOWED ME ONE OF THE TOYS THAT DEAR MISS MORTON HAD KNOCKED TOGETHER FROM OLD TIMBERS.

"BELIEVE ME, FOR A FOUR YEAR OLD, IT
WAS CERTAINLY QUITE IMPRESSIVE."

Chapter Thirteen

MOONLIGHT, MURDER AND MAYHEM

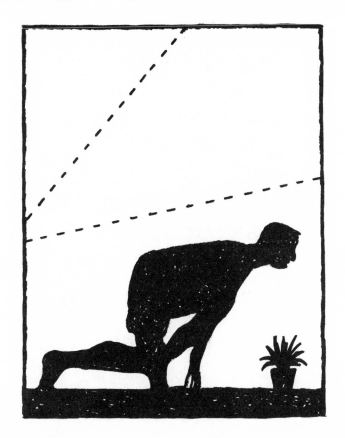

380 Riverside Drive, N.Y.C.
28th October 1951, 12.15 p.m.

ROMANCE CONTINUED TO
BLOSSOM FOR GLADYS.
SHE RECEIVED AN
INVITATION FROM ART
COLLECTOR CARTER
DUHAMEL TO JOIN HIM
FOR LUNCH AT HIS
RIVERSIDE DRIVE
APARTMENT. SHE ARRIVED
AT THE APPOINTED HOUR,
BUT SUDDENLY FOUND
HERSELF PLUNGED INTO
CIRCUMSTANCES THAT
WERE SOMEWHAT
DISCONCERTING...

GLADYS HAD NOT REALIZED

THAT LUNCH WOULD BE A FORMAL AFFAIR.

THEY BEGAN TO MEET ON A REGULAR
BASIS. THEN, ONE EVENING AFTER
DINNER, HE INVITED GLADYS BACK
FOR A NIGHTCAP. IT SOON BECAME
APPARENT, HOWEVER, THAT MR.
DUHAMEL HAD MORE ON HIS MIND
THAN THE VIEW OVER THE HUDSON
RIVER. HE PRESSED HIS BODY UP
CLOSE AS HE WHISPERED IN HER
EAR ABOUT HIS SEARCH FOR LOVE IN
A LONELY, UNCARING WORLD. GLADYS,
ALTHOUGH BORED PRACTICALLY TO
TEARS, MANAGED TO REMAIN AWAKE,
BUT SOON FOUND THAT

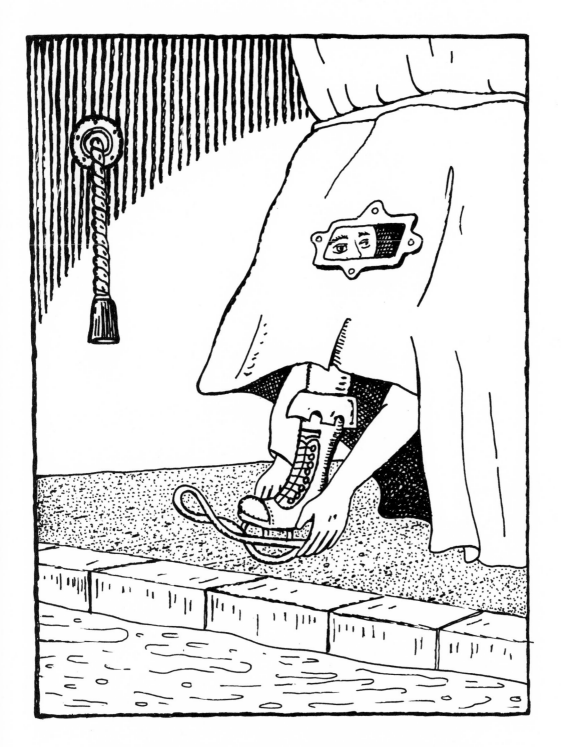

MR. DUHAMEL HAD SOME STRANGE
IDEAS ABOUT FOREPLAY.

ON HER NEXT VISIT TO
HIS APARTMENT, GLADYS
BEGAN TO REALIZE THERE
WAS SOMETHING SLIGHTLY
UNNERVING ABOUT HER
SOPHISTICATED COMPANION.
HER WORST FEARS WERE
REALIZED WHEN SHE
UNLOCKED THE DOOR TO
HIS STUDY AND LEARNED
ABOUT THE DARKER SIDE
OF CARTER DUHAMEL.
GLADYS GASPED.

A FASCINATION WITH GOURDS MARRED
AN OTHERWISE CHEERFUL DISPOSITION.

UNFORTUNATELY, THIS WAS TO BE THE
LAST STRAW. THEIR RELATIONSHIP CAME
TO AN END TWO NIGHTS LATER, IN THE
KITCHEN OF HIS APARTMENT.
THE BODY WAS DISCOVERED BY THE
CLEANING WOMAN ON FRIDAY MORNING AT 11.25.

MULHEARDY'S MEN

WERE SOON

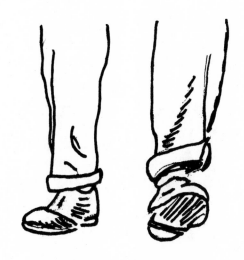

ON THE CASE

WHILST GLADYS WAS ON
THE TOWN...

...MEETING YOUNG MEN WHO SEEMED
DETERMINED TO IMPRESS AT ANY COST.

GLADYS SOUGHT OUT
A YOUNG HUNGARIAN
AVIATOR SHE HAD MET
AT THE CEDAR BAR.
HIS INVITATION TO
ELOPE –

"COME FLY WITH ME"–
SHE FELT OBLIGED
TO DECLINE.

HOWEVER, SHE DID
PERSUADE HIM TO PART
WITH $ 2000.

BEFORE TELEPHONING
HER FIANCÉ, THEODORE
BAHNWEILER. "DARLING,
WE SIMPLY MUST FLEE
THESE DISMAL PARTS,"
SHE BLURTED.
THE NEXT THREE DAYS
WERE WITNESS TO FRANTIC
ACTIVITY ACROSS
MANHATTAN.

THEODORE BAHNWEILER PACKED TEN
SUITCASES; TYLER GRANTHE DECLARED HIS
UNDYING LOVE FOR GLADYS; TRUBCOCK
TASTED HIS FIRST CHEESEBURGER;
GLADYS ENLISTED THE ASSISTANCE OF TWO
SMALLTIME HOODLUMS, GINZETTI AND
MOLLONE, AND TUCKED A SPANNER INTO
HER KILT.

ON SATURDAY 10th NOVEMBER AT MIDNIGHT,
THE BAHNWEILER PROTOTYPE DIRIGIBLE
VIIB SLIPPED ITS MOORING AT LAKEHURST.

THE FIVE PASSENGERS WATCHED THE
LIGHTS OF NEW JERSEY RECEDE INTO
THE MURK.

SUDDENLY, THE TWIN HEADLIGHTS OF A CHECKER CAB PIERCED THE GLOOM BELOW.

"IT'S McNALLY!" CRIED TYLER GRANTHE.

"LOWER THE ROPE LADDER!" HE SCRAMBLED DOWN TO THE TARMAC AND RACED TO THE CAB, PAID THE DRIVER AND RETURNED WITH McNALLY TO THE GONDOLA OF THE AIRSHIP.

"HOW ON EARTH DID THE CAB BRING THE ROBOT OUT TO LAKEHURST?" GROWLED GINZETTI.

"IT'S ONLY BROOKLYN THEY DON'T
GO," INTERRUPTED GLADYS.
"I MEAN, HOW DID THE ROBOT KNOW
YOU WUZ HERE?" GINZETTI ADDED.
"CONSTANT RADIO CONTACT...

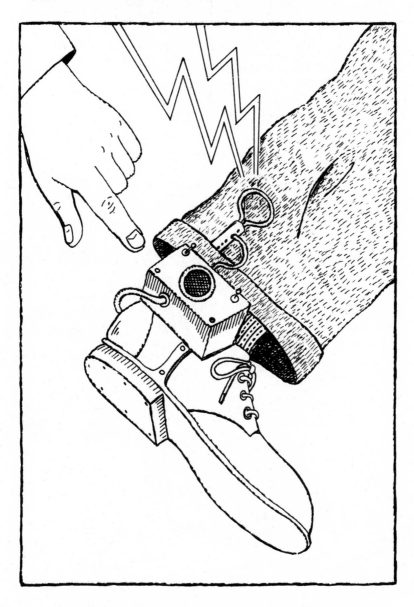

...HERE," REPLIED GRANTHE.

DETECTIVE INSPECTOR MULHEARDY HAD
NOT BEEN SLEEPING AT ALL WELL OF LATE.
STRANGE IMAGES HAD BEGUN TO DRIFT

THROUGH HIS SUBCONSCIOUS WANDERINGS.

THE HEADLINES IN THE MORNING PAPERS
BROUGHT NO RELIEF...

AFTER ANOTHER
EXHAUSTING DAY
MAKING ENQUIRIES
DOWNTOWN, TRUBCOCK
AND MULHEARDY
SOUGHT REFUGE IN
BOTH GRAPE AND
GRAIN.
THE ENGLISHMAN
SOON FOUND HIMSELF
EXPERIENCING NEW
SENSATIONS OF
TOTAL RELAXATION.

EIGHTH AVENUE BEGAN TO LOOK
DECIDEDLY DIFFERENT.

Chapter Fourteen

THE ARREST OF A SUSPECT

Apt. 18, 437 East 12th Street,
New York City, 12th November
1951, 11·45 a.m.

SORGOR ARVIDSSON WOKE UP
AND LOOKED AT THE CLOCK.

HE WAS STILL HAVING PROBLEMS
WITH IT. HE WAS NOT UNDULY
WORRIED, HOWEVER, FOR TODAY
HE HAD BEEN SUMMONED TO THE
RESIDENCE OF TYLER GRANTHE
TO DISCUSS WORK ON AN
EXCITING NEW PROJECT.
"TYLER GRANTHE, ONE OF THE
TOP INVENTORS IN MANHATTAN!
AT LAST MY GENIUS WILL BE
RECOGNIZED!"

HE ARRIVED AT THE GRANTHE
MANSION AT PRECISELY 8.20
AND RANG THE BELL.

A DISTRAUGHT MRS GRANTHE
OPENED THE DOOR.

"HE LEFT ME!" SHE CRIED.

"BUT I HAVE MANY PLANS,"
BLURTED SORGOR.

"PERHAPS WE COULD DISCUSS
THEM...DOWNTOWN."

HE FELT A FIRM HAND ON HIS
SHOULDER AND TURNED TO FACE THE
SPEAKER, DETECTIVE MULHEARDY.

Chapter Fifteen

OVER THE BAY

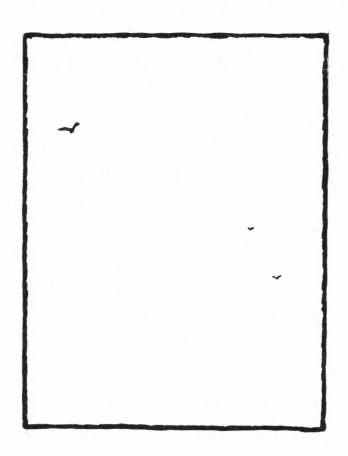

San Francisco, C.A, Saturday
2ⁿᵈ December 1951 , 7.29 a.m

THE PRISONERS CROSSING THE
EXERCISE YARD AT ALCATRAZ
LOOKED UP AT THE STRANGE CRAFT
CIRCLING THE BAY.
"WHAT IS THAT INTERESTING
LITTLE ISLAND DOWN THERE?"
ENQUIRED GLADYS AS MᶜNALLY
POURED FRESH COFFEE ON TO HER
SHOES.

"I'M TAKING HER DOWN OVER
MARIN COUNTY," ANNOUNCED
BAHNWEILER. "I'VE MADE
RESERVATIONS AT THE CASA
MADRONA."

"PERHAPS THEY HAVE
SHOE-DRYING FACILITIES THERE,"
NOTED GLADYS ICILY.

THE TRAVELLERS SPENT FOUR
HAPPY DAYS IN CALIFORNIA.
  SIGHTSEEING OCCUPIED MOST
OF THEIR TIME.
  BUT WHEREAS MOST TOURISTS
WERE QUITE CONTENT TO DRIVE
THE FAMILY CAR THROUGH THE
GIANT SEQUOIAS, GLADYS
PREFERRED TO DO THINGS "IN THE
MORTON MANNER"...

HOWEVER, THIS MOMENTARY EUPHORIA WAS
SHATTERED THE FOLLOWING MORNING AT
BREAKFAST BY THE ARRIVAL OF THE PAPERS...

"ANYTHING WRONG?" ASKED THEODORE.

"YOU SEEM SO PALE."
GLADYS FOLDED THE NEWSPAPER AND
REACHED FOR THE COFFEE.
"ARE YOU FOLLOWING THE BILLIARD
TABLE MURDERS?" HER FIANCÉ ENQUIRED.
"BOTH FASCINATING AND HORRIBLE."
"I THINK NOT," SNAPPED GLADYS.
"WELL, I'M AFRAID I HAVE ONLY BAD
NEWS, MY DEAR. THE BANKER'S TRUST
HAVE WIRED THIS MORNING. I'M
BANKRUPT, RUINED. COULD YOU STILL
MARRY A MAN WHO HAS LOST
EVERYTHING?"
"OF COURSE," CHIMED IN GLADYS.
"AND TONIGHT YOU AND I WILL
CELEBRATE WITH A MEAL IN YOUR
ROOM. I'LL COOK."

TWO HOURS LATER, THE BRIGHT
YELLOW TRUCK BEARING A BRAND
NEW BILLIARD TABLE CROSSED THE
BAY BRIDGE, HEADING EAST.

AFTER SUPPER GLADYS SLIPPED
AWAY TO A RENDEZVOUS WITH TYLER
GRANTHE ON THE BALCONY.

"LUCY, PLEASE RECONSIDER YOUR
ENGAGEMENT TO BAHNWEILER," HE
IMPLORED.

"I HAVE. IT'S YOU I WANT,"
WHISPERED GLADYS.

"DEAREST LUCY, WILL OUR LOVE
TRULY NEVER DIE?"

"IT IS WRITTEN IN THE STARS,
MY LOVE," BEAMED GLADYS.

"DARLING TYLER, THEODORE IS HISTORY. LET US FLY DOWN TO RIO TONIGHT AND TIE THE KNOT."

"LUCY, I'M IN HEAVEN," ANNOUNCED THE INVENTOR, "I'LL TELL THE BOYS TO MAKE THE AIRSHIP READY."

GINZETTI AND MOLLONE RELEASED THE CABLE, ALLOWING THE AIRSHIP TO RISE GRACEFULLY INTO THE CALIFORNIAN DAWN. McNALLY PUTTERED TO AND FRO SPILLING FRESH COFFEE ON TO THE FLOOR.

GLADYS AND HER NEW LOVE TURNED TO THE HORIZON.

"RIO, HERE WE COME!" THEY BOTH CRIED.

"GINZETTI, DID YOU BRING THE MAP?" ASKED GLADYS.
"RIGHT HERE, BOSS."

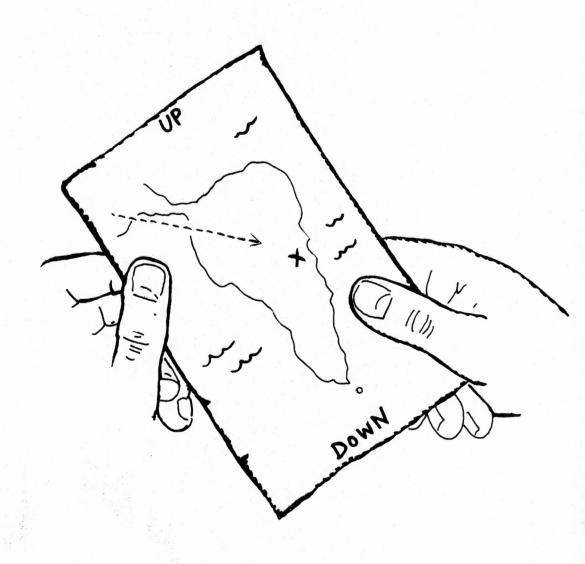

GLADYS REALIZED THAT IT MIGHT NOT TURN OUT TO BE SUCH AN EASY JOURNEY AFTER ALL.

Chapter Sixteen
A SUDDEN MOVE

Room 211 , 10th Precinct
N.Y.P.D. Manhattan , 6th
December , 11. 36 a.m.

DETECTIVE TRUBCOCK AND MULHEARDY
WERE HAVING PROBLEMS WITH THEIR
MAIN SUSPECT, SORGOR ARVIDSSON.
"JUST WHAT WERE YOU DOING AT THE
GRANTHE RESIDENCE?" THUNDERED
MULHEARDY.
"I CALL ABOUT SPONGE EMPIRE," REPLIED
ARVIDSSON.
"WHAT DO YOU KNOW ABOUT ITALIAN
FOOD?" RASPED TRUBCOCK.
"THE FUTURE IS IN SPONGE," BLURTED
THE SUSPECT.
THE TELEPHONE RANG. TRUBCOCK
SWITCHED THE LIGHT BACK ON
AND PICKED UP THE RECEIVER.

"THAT YOU, MULHEARDY? DETECTIVE
SERGEANT WALKER HERE, SAN FRANCISCO
HOMICIDE. WE'VE JUST GOT A REPORT
IN ON SOME GUY OUT IN MARIN COUNTY.
FOUND HIM FACE DOWN IN THE
CANNELLONI. THINGS IS LOOKING UP!"

TWO HOURS LATER, ARVIDSSON WAS
RELEASED, AND TRUBCOCK AND MULHEARDY
SET OUT, HEADING WEST. IN HIS RIGHT
HAND THE ENGLISHMAN GRIPPED THE BRAND
NEW FOOD ANALYSER — A GIFT FROM FORENSIC.

Chapter Seventeen
LUNCH

The Kitchen "The Beeches",
Lower Biddlington, Kent
6th December 1951, midnight

EDNA TRUBCOCK LOVINGLY STIRRED THE
BURNT CABBAGE SOUP. IT WAS SOMETHING
OF A SPECIALITY IN THE TRUBCOCK HOUSE.

A LARGE VAN PULLED UP SHARPLY IN THE
DRIVE. LARGE RED LETTERS ON THE SIDE
PROCLAIMED: "DAMARROIDS:
THE GREAT REJUVENATOR."
THE TELEPHONE RANG. SHE STOPPED
STIRRING, AND AS THE SPOON SANK BENEATH
THE SURFACE, PICKED UP THE RECEIVER.

Chapter Eighteen
THE CHASE IS ON

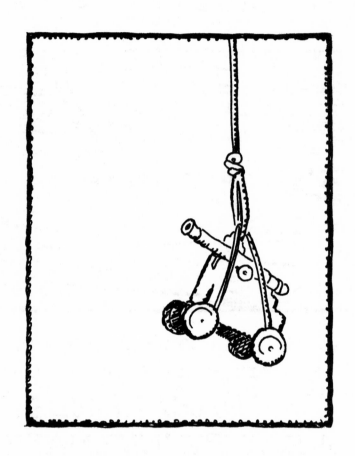

San Pablo Ave. San Francisco,
California, 8th December 1951
11.38 a.m.

ON THEIR ARRIVAL IN CALIFORNIA,
TRUBCOCK AND MULHEARDY HEADED STRAIGHT
OUT THROUGH BERKELEY TO EL CERRITO.

"WE'RE CHECKED IN AT THE BRANTLEY KEARNS LODGE", SAID MULHEARDY TO HIS ENGLISH COMPANION. TOMORROW WE'LL SPEAK TO THE MANAGER OF THE CASA MADRONA, BUT TONIGHT LET'S SAMPLE SOME CALIFORNIAN HOSPITALITY."

9.15 a.m. THE CASA MADRONA HOTEL, MARIN COUNTY.

"WE'RE LOOKING FOR A CERTAIN PARTY WHO CHECKED IN FROM NEW YORK."

"AH YES," SAID THE MANAGER. "THE EAST COAST PARTY. ONE OF WHOM I SEEM TO RECALL WAS SOMEWHAT TINNISH."

"YOU MEAN TINNISH, AS IN METAL?" INTERRUPTED TRUBCOCK.

"YES, I WOULD SAY THAT HE WAS, IN FACT, ALMOST TOTALLY TINNISH."

"ARE YOU TRYING TO TELL ME THIS GUY WAS A GODDAM ROBOT?" YELLED MULHEARDY.

"ONE DOESN'T LIKE TO REVEAL TOO MUCH OF THE PERSONAL HABITS OF ONE'S CLIENTELE. A CERTAIN DEGREE OF DISCRETION IS..."

" I'D LIKE TO REMIND YOU THIS IS A HOMICIDE CASE", BARKED MULHEARDY. "NOW TELL US WHERE THEY ARE."

"WELL, THE BELLHOP DID OVERHEAR THEM TALKING ABOUT SOUTH AMERICA".

Chapter Nineteen
AERIAL REVELATIONS

The U.S.- Mexican Border
6th December 1951, 7.26 p.m.

AS THE AIRSHIP NOSED SOUTH, TYLER GRANTHE REALIZED THAT ROMANTIC CANDLELIT SUPPERS HIGH ABOVE THE CLOUDS WITH HIS TRUE LOVE WERE BEGINNING TO LOSE SOME OF THEIR APPEAL, ESPECIALLY WHEN Mc NALLY INSISTED NOT ONLY ON PREPARING THE FOOD BUT ALSO ON DEMONSTRATING THE GENOVESE TECHNIQUE FOR EATING CALZONE WITH A MIXED PEPPER SALAD.

"OPUS EST OLIO!" THUNDERED McNALLY.

AS TYLER GRANTHE RAISED ANOTHER
"HOBOKEN TREMBLER" TO HIS LIPS, GLADYS
LEANED OVER TOWARDS HIM.

"TYLER, MY LOVE, WERE THERE MANY OTHER WOMEN IN YOUR LIFE?" WHISPERED GLADYS.

"ONLY REBECCA. WE MET AT A SPIKE JONES CONCERT, FELL IN LOVE AND WERE MARRIED WITHIN TWO MONTHS. UNFORTUNATELY, THINGS BEGAN TO GO DOWNHILL ON THE NIGHT OF OUR HONEYMOON."

"IT DIDN'T WORK OUT, THEN?"

"I'M AFRAID NOT. REBECCA PROVED TO BE SOMETHING OF AN ENIGMA..."

"NOW THAT I'VE MET YOU, MY
LOVE, I FEEL LIKE A NEW MAN.

I WANT TO GO ON AND CONQUER
THE WORLD, TO SURPASS EVEN
THE OUTSTANDING ACHIEVEMENTS
OF DEAR OLIVER."

"OLIVER?" MURMURED GLADYS.
"YOU NEVER MENTIONED HIM
BEFORE, IS HE..."

"HE WAS MY ELDER BROTHER.
TALL, STRONG, INTELLIGENT,
SHINING LIKE A BEACON IN A
MURKY, CYNICAL WORLD OF
EXISTENTIALIST WASTRELS."

" WHAT AN INSPIRATION TO US ALL
HE WAS, DEAR OLIVER.
MY BROTHER WAS AN EXTRA-
ORDINARY MAN.
THERE WAS NO CHALLENGE IN
THE WORLD TOO GREAT FOR HIM.

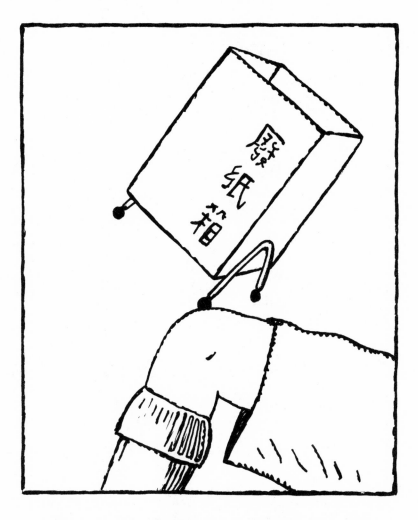

HE HAD CIRCLED THE GLOBE
TWICE BEFORE HIS TWENTIETH
BIRTHDAY.

HE WAS ALWAYS PUSHING HIMSELF TO
THE LIMITS OF HUMAN ENDURANCE.

"HE WAS AN EXPERT
SWORDSMAN, POLO-PLAYER,
PRIZE-WINNING POET,
FLAUTIST AND RACONTEUR.
  AT THE AGE OF TWENTY-SIX
HE BECAME FASCINATED BY
THE AFRICAN LANDSCAPE,
TRAVELLING OUT THERE TO
OBSERVE AND RECORD THE
WONDROUS DIVERSITY OF
FLORA AND FAUNA. HIS
PICTORIAL SURVEY 'ON THE
BANKS OF THE MIGHTY
LIMPOPO' ACHIEVED WORLD-
WIDE ACCLAIM.

"HIS CAREER IN WILDLIFE PHOTOGRAPHY WAS, HOWEVER, SHORT-LIVED."

"AND THEN?" ASKED GLADYS.
TYLER'S THIRD "TREMBLER" OF THE
EVENING CRASHED TO THE FLOOR.
   "TURBULENCE!" HE CRIED. "TAKE
HER UP, McNALLY, WE'RE RUNNING
INTO A STORM!"
   THE AUTHORITIES AT DAKAR
REPORTED NEWS OF THE WRECKAGE
SOME TWO WEEKS LATER.

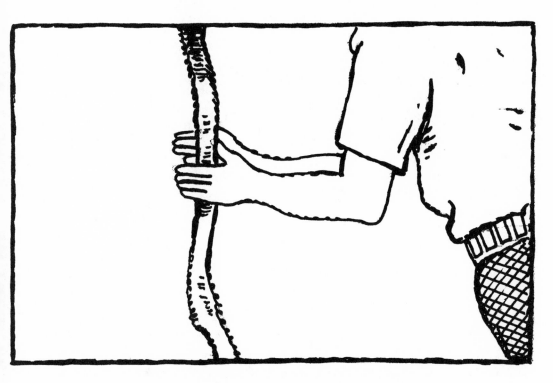

NO BODIES WERE FOUND.

Chapter Twenty
MESSAGE FROM BEYOND

Taylor Street, San Francisco
10th December 1951 , 11.14 p.m.

THAT EVENING TRUBCOCK AND
MULHEARDY WERE ONCE AGAIN
SITTING DESPONDENTLY IN A BAR
DOWNTOWN WHEN THE BARMAN
LEANED OVER AND HANDED THEM A
COPY OF THE OAKLAND TRIBUNE.
"YOU GUYS NEED A BREAK IN THIS
BILLIARD CASE. MAYBE YOU SHOULD
CONTACT PRENTISS FULSTOCK, THE
PSYCHIC. HE CLAIMS HE CAN FIND
ANYBODY!"

MULHEARDY LOOKED DOWN AT THE
SMALL AD.

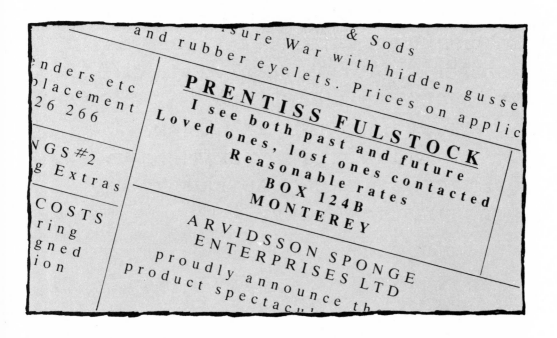

"COME ON, MULHEARDY," SAID TRUBCOCK.
"IT'S WORTH A SHOT."

TURNING LEFT OFF THE HIGHWAY,
THEY STOPPED AT A SMALL FRUIT
STAND. THE PROPRIETOR ANSWERED
THEIR QUESTIONS SOMEWHAT GRUFFLY.
 "THE OLD FULSTOCK PLACE ? DON'T
GET MANY FOLKS GOING UP THERE
THESE DAYS, LEASTWISE NOT AFTER
DARK."
 "SHOULD WE THEREFORE EXERCISE A
DEGREE OF CAUTION UPON ARRIVAL?"
ENQUIRED TRUBCOCK.
 "YEP, REPLIED THE OLD WOMAN.
TWENTY MINUTES LATER THE TWO
DETECTIVES DREW CAUTIOUSLY INTO
THE FULSTOCK DRIVE.

FULSTOCK WAS KNOWN NOT TO TAKE
KINDLY TOWARDS TRESPASSERS.

HE STEPPED FROM BEHIND THE
CANNON, ADJUSTED HIS TOUPEE
AND ANNOUNCED :

"I DON'T NORMALLY APPRECIATE
PERSONAL CALLERS, GENTLEMEN,
BUT THELMA RANG FROM THE FRUIT
STAND. SHE RECOGNIZED YOU FROM
YOUR PICTURE IN THE OAKLAND·
TRIBUNE. DETECTIVES MOORHOUSE
AND TRIPCOT, I BELIEVE..."

"CLOSE", SNAPPED MULHEARDY.
" CAN WE TALK INSIDE ?"

SEATED IN THE KITCHEN, THE DETECTIVES SPOKE OF THEIR MISSION.

"THE PERSON YOU SEEK IS FAR AWAY. THE BIG SHIP IS GONE. I SEE A MIGHTY CONTINENT IN THE CLOUDS. THAT'LL BE FIFTY DOLLARS, PAYABLE NOW," RESPONDED THE CLAIRVOYANT.

THEY PAID UP AND DROVE BACK TO SAN FRANCISCO.

"YOU KNOW," SAID MULHEARDY, "I HAVE A FEELING THEY PLANNED THEIR GETAWAY RIGHT DOWN TO THE LAST DETAIL."*

* SEE MAP ON PAGE 146

"ARE YOU COMING HOME FOR CHRISTMAS, DEAR?"

TRUBCOCK FROZE. A VISION OF CHARRED FOWL FLICKERED THROUGH HIS MIND, FOLLOWED IMMEDIATELY BY AN IMAGE OF A MOUND OF GREENISH LUMPS WHICH MIGHT CONCEIVABLY BE THE REMAINS OF SPROUTS.

"EDNA, I'M AFRAID SOMETHING HAS CROPPED UP. WE HAVE A LEAD IN THE MORTON CASE THAT TAKES ME TO AFRICA. IT'S ALMOST OVER."

"YOU SAID THAT TWO MONTHS AGO," SNAPPED MRS. TRUBCOCK. SHE SLAMMED DOWN THE RECEIVER AND PICKED UP A RUSTY EGG WHISK.

TRUBCOCK DRUMMED HIS FINGERS ON THE DIAL. OUTSIDE, THE FOG SEEMED TO BE LIFTING. HE WAS JUST ABOUT ABLE TO MAKE OUT THE NEON SIGN OF THE FLYING HAND DINER ON THE HIGHWAY OUT TO THE AIRPORT.

"LOOKS O.K. NOW," SAID MULHEARDY. TRUBCOCK SHOOK HANDS AND SAID GOODBYE TO HIS COLLEAGUE, AND LEFT TO CATCH HIS PLANE.

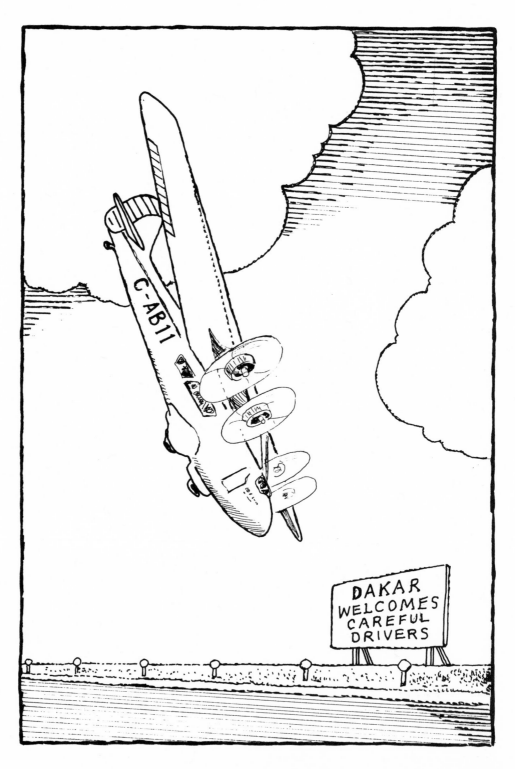

HE ARRIVED IN AFRICA EIGHTEEN HOURS LATER.

176

Chapter Twenty One
DESTINATION DAKAR

The Beach, Dakar, Senegal,
West Africa, 29ᵃ April 1952, 11·45 p.m.

"WE MADE IT!" EXCLAIMED GLADYS.
Mc NALLY TOTTERED ACROSS THE BEACH,
CLANKING AND SQUEAKING.
"IT WAS A STRANGE DECISION OF THE
OTHERS TO LEAP AS WE APPROACHED
TERRA FIRMA!"
"OH, I DON'T KNOW," QUIPPED GLADYS,
TUCKING HER LUGER BACK INTO HER
BLOUSE. "NOW LET'S GET OUT OF HERE
BEFORE PEOPLE START ASKING
AWKWARD QUESTIONS. WE NEED TO BLEND
INTO THE BACKGROUND."

UPON HIS ARRIVAL IN DAKAR, DETECTIVE INSPECTOR TRUBCOCK WAS PRESENTED WITH A TELEGRAM:

DARLING MISS YOU STOP LONGING FOR DINNER TOGETHER STOP BE HOME SOON STOP LOVE EDNA

SCOTLAND YARD HAD BEGUN TO RECEIVE DISTURBING NEWS. PIERRE BODIN, AN INTERNATIONAL DIAMOND DEALER, HAD BEEN FOUND DEAD IN HIS LUXURY BUNGALOW ON 3rd MAY 1952. THAT SAME DAY THE THEFT OF THE ONLY BILLIARD TABLE IN DAKAR WAS REPORTED AT THE HEADQUARTERS OF THE WESTERN SENEGAL PHILATELIC SOCIETY. ROADBLOCKS WERE BEING PLACED ON EVERY ROAD LEADING OUT OF TOWN.

TRUBCOCK'S SUPERIORS AT SCOTLAND
YARD SENSED THAT A CONCLUSION TO
THE MORTON CASE WAS CLOSE AT HAND.

A TEAM OF HIGHLY EXPERIENCED
OFFICERS WAS DISPATCHED FROM A TOP-
SECRET NAVAL BASE ON THE SOUTH
COAST, THEIR DESTINATION DAKAR.

Chapter Twenty Two
PERILOUS JOURNEY

The Basement, Hotel Larbaud,
Dakar, 5th May 1952, 9.12 a.m.

GLADYS, SOMEWHAT ANNOYED BY THE
INCREASING POLICE ACTIVITY, PACKED
A SUITCASE, OILED Mc NALLY AND
ARRANGED FOR TRANSPORT TO BE MADE
AVAILABLE.

Mc NALLY APPEARED WITH A LONG
STEEL PIPE, WELDING EQUIPMENT
AND THE OCTOBER 1948 EDITION OF
"PRACTICAL MECHANICS".

THREE HOURS LATER, THEY WERE
LEAVING TOWN...

... WITH INSPECTOR TRUBCOCK IN HOT PURSUIT.

IT PROVED TO BE A GRUELLING
JOURNEY ACROSS FORBIDDEN TERRAIN,
HEADING NORTH TO KIFFA, SNATCHING
MEALS HERE AND THERE BEFORE
CONTINUING HIS MISSION TO BRING
GLADYS BABBINGTON MORTON TO JUSTICE.

HE LEFT EL KSAIB OUNANE AT DAWN
AND PLODDED NORTH BY NORTH-EAST.

OCCASIONALLY HIS BRAIN BECAME
HAUNTED BY THE SPECTRE OF YARDS OF
CANNELLONI TUBES ROLLING DOWNHILL
TOWARDS HIS NAKED BODY. HE TRIED
DESPERATELY TO RID HIS MIND OF THE
TERROR AND SPURRED HIS MOUNT ON
TO THE NEXT STOP AT IN SALAH. HERE
HE SNATCHED A FEW HOURS' SLEEP, THEN
SET OUT FOR TOUGGOURT VIA MIRIBEL.

187

THE SPECIAL TASK FORCE WAS
MOVING EVER NEARER, PLOTTING
A COURSE ROUGHLY PARALLEL TO
THE IBERIAN PENINSULA. IN ORDER
TO PRESERVE MORALE AND MAINTAIN
A HIGH STANDARD OF FITNESS AND
AWARENESS, REGULAR MOCK
INVESTIGATIONS WERE HELD IN THE
KITCHEN QUARTERS, PAYING SPECIAL
ATTENTION TO THE TRACING AND
ANALYSING OF RANDOM SCRAPS OF FOOD.

BY THE END OF THREE DAYS OF
INTENSIVE INVESTIGATION, THE FORCE
WAS CONFIDENT THAT THEY COULD
IN FACT TACKLE AND ANALYSE ANY
CUISINE THAT WAS THROWN AT THEM.

Chapter Twenty Three
TRUBCOCK DROPS IN

Touggourt, North Africa
Tuesday 28th October 1952, 11.55 a.m

INSPECTOR TRUBCOCK FOUND HIMSELF
FACE TO FACE WITH THE LOCAL
RADIOGRAPHER IN TOUGGOURT PLAZA.
"YES. I SEE WOMAN AND METAL MAN.

SHE WAS EXACTLY THIS TALL, IN COURT
SHOES. THEY TOOK VEGETABLE TRUCK
AND LIT OUT FOR MAHDIA, ON COAST."

TRUBCOCK PERSUADED AN UNEMPLOYED
PLUMBER TO FLY HIM UP TO THE COAST ON
WHAT HE HOPED WOULD BE THE LAST
LEG OF HIS JOURNEY.

AFTER FOURTEEN HOURS OF FLYING,
TRUBCOCK NOTICED A DUST CLOUD
MOVING SLOWLY UP A HILL BELOW.

PEERING DOWN, HE SAW A VEGETABLE
TRUCK RATTLING ALONG THE ROUGH
TRACK. HE GRIPPED HIS FOOD ANALYSER
AND TAPPED THE PLUMBER THREE
TIMES ON THE HEAD.

"I'M GOING DOWN!" SPLUTTERED TRUBCOCK.

GLADYS LOOKED IN THE REAR-VIEW
MIRROR AND THROUGH THE CLOUDS OF
DUST WAS JUST ABLE TO MAKE OUT
A TINY BLUR OF WHITE AND BROWN
THAT GRADUALLY SHE BEGAN TO
RECOGNIZE AS A PARACHUTE.

"WHAT'S THAT, McNALLY?" SHE SHOUTED
TO HER COMPANION.
"SCOTLAND BARD," SQUEAKED BACK
McNALLY.
"THEY'RE SMARTER THAN I THOUGHT,"
HISSED GLADYS AS HER FOOT HIT
THE ACCELERATOR.

Chapter Twenty Four
NO SIGN OF DUDLEY

The Kitchen, "The Beeches",
Lower Biddlington, Kent
Sunday 8th December 1952, 7.29 pm

"YES, THIS IS MRS. TRUBCOCK SPEAKING.
I'LL PAY FOR THE CALL. PUT HIM THROUGH."

"EDNA, MY LOVE. I'M IN HOSPITAL IN TUNIS. I'VE BROKEN MY RIGHT LEG. I'VE LOST MISS MORTON THIS TIME, BUT WE'RE RIGHT ON HER TAIL NOW."

"DARLING, I CAN HARDLY WAIT FOR YOUR RETURN. YOU'LL SEE ALL MY NEW KITCHEN APPLIANCES. WE HAVE A REFRIGERATOR NOW."

THERE WAS A MUFFLED GROAN DOWN THE LINE, THEN A STRANGE VOICE SAID, "DOCTOR DIDIER SEMIN HERE. I'M AFRAID YOUR HUSBAND HAS COLLAPSED. HE WILL CALL AGAIN, PERHAPS TOMORROW."

THE LIGHTS OF MAHDIA HARBOUR
FADED BEYOND THE WAKE OF THE
TINY FISHING BOAT THAT HAD BEEN
STOLEN BY GLADYS AND MCNALLY.

SEEING INSPECTOR TRUBCOCK PARACHUTE
INTO THE RAVINE JUST SIXTEEN FEET
BEHIND HER TRUCK HAD ALERTED GLADYS
TO THE GRAVITY OF HER SITUATION IN AFRICA.
SHE HAD SPENT VERY LITTLE TIME IN
MAHDIA, PAUSING ONLY TO SECURE A SUPPLY OF
FOOD, DRINK AND MACHINE-OIL FOR MCNALLY.

BY A STROKE OF FORTUNE SHE HAD BEEN
ABLE TO SNAP UP THE ONLY BILLIARD
TABLE IN TOWN AT A BARGAIN PRICE,

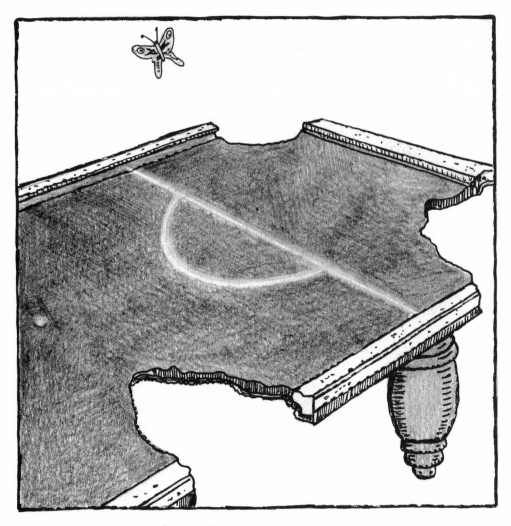

OWING TO SOME SLIGHT DAMAGE TO
THE POCKETS WREAKED BY THE DEADLY
SUDANESE GREEN EMPEROR MOTH.
NOW THEY WERE SAILING NORTH
WITH THEIR PRECIOUS CARGO. GLADYS
LEANED BACK AND LIT UP ANOTHER CIGAR.

TRUBCOCK HOBBLED OVER TO THE HOSPITAL
WINDOW. HE LOOKED DOWN AT THE WORLD OUTSIDE.

NOTHING HAD CHANGED.

AN EGYPTIAN NURSE SHUFFLED UP TO
THE DETECTIVE INSPECTOR AND ANNOUNCED,
"HERE IS THE REPORT FROM THE ITALIAN
AUTHORITIES!"

NAPLES, TUESDAY
WE HAVE REPORTED SIGHTINGS
OF A YOUNG WOMAN AND A
METAL OBJECT ANSWERING
TO YOUR DESCRIPTION, IN
PALERMO ON THE 15TH,
COSENZA IN CALABRIA
ON THE 20TH,
PERUGIA ON THE 26TH AND
RAVENNA ON THE 30TH
— VAN KOOTEN

FOR THE FIRST TIME IN THREE YEARS,
TRUBCOCK ALLOWED HIMSELF A SMILE.
"I MAY YET MISS ANOTHER CHRISTMAS
DINNER", HE MURMURED.

Chapter Twenty Five
McNALLY DUCKS OUT

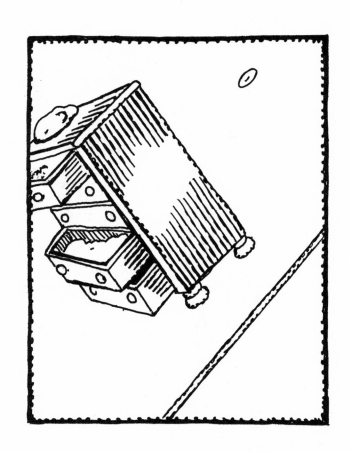

Room 18ᴮ, Locanda Montin,
San Trovaso, Venice, Monday
26ᵗʰ February 1957, 3.15 a.m.

GLADYS TURNED TO Mc NALLY AND SAID,
"THE SITUATION IS SERIOUS, Mc NALLY.
ACCORDING TO THE NEWSPAPERS THIS
INSPECTOR TRIBCUTT IS DETERMINED TO
MEET US. THAT MUST NOT HAPPEN. DO
YOU UNDERSTAND?"

"ECCE TRIBCUTTI", RASPED Mc NALLY.
"YOU ARE NOT TO LEAVE YOUR ROOM
UNTIL I SAY. IS THAT CLEAR? SECRECY
IS IMPERATIVE!"

GLADYS DREW THE SHUTTERS IN HER
ROOM, SAT DOWN AND RAISED A CIGAR
TO HER LIPS.

FROM HER ROOM, GLADYS SAW VERY LITTLE
OF THE SPLENDOURS OF VENICE.

UNFORTUNATELY, Mc NALLY COULD NOT
CONTAIN HIMSELF, AND AFTER LUNCH
HE SLIPPED DOWNSTAIRS AND OUT INTO
THE STREET. HE LUMBERED DOWN TO
THE GRAND CANAL, WHERE HE MANAGED
TO SQUEAK OUT A FEW WORDS OF LATIN
TO THE BEMUSED GONDOLIER WHO WAS
LOITERING ON THE QUAY. WITHIN A
MATTER OF MINUTES Mc NALLY WAS
BEING TRANSPORTED ALONG THE
GRAND CANAL TOWARDS SAN MARCO.

DETECTIVE INSPECTOR TRUBCOCK NOTICED THE
METALLIC GLEAM FROM THE RIALTO CAFÉ.

IT WAS THE BREAK HE HAD PRAYED
FOR MANY TIMES OVER THE YEARS.
PUSHING ASIDE HIS CAPPUCCINO, HE RAN
DOWN TO THE WATER'S EDGE WHERE
HE SAW THE GREEN AND GOLD LAUNCH
MOORED BY TWO SLENDER ROPES. HE
PAUSED BY THE LETTERS S.A. WROUGHT
INTO THE PROW, THEN JUMPED ABOARD,
CAST OFF AND STARTED THE ENGINE.
  THE SPONGE PROW SURGED FORWARD.
"HEY! COME BACK! THAT'S MISTER
ARVIDSSON'S PRIVATE LAUNCH!" WERE
THE LAST WORDS HE HEARD BEFORE
CUTTING DOWN THE CANAL.

MᶜNALLY TURNED, SAW THE POWERFUL LAUNCH
SURGING TOWARDS HIM AND STIFFENED.

FEARFUL OF THE WRATH OF HIS MISTRESS,
HE DECIDED ON IMMEDIATE ACTION.

TRUBCOCK DREW ALONGSIDE AND
SHOUTED AT THE STARTLED GONDOLIER,
"WHERE METAL MEN COME FROM?"
THE GONDOLIER WIPED HIS KNITTED
BROW AND SHOUTED BACK,
"ACTUALLY I PICKED UP THE GENTLEMAN
IN FRONT OF THE ACCADEMIA. I PRESUMED
THAT, LIKE SO MANY AMERICANS, HE
WAS STAYING AT THE LOCANDA MONTIN."
"THANK YOU, MY WATERBORNE FRIEND,"
WHISPERED TRUBCOCK. HE STARTED UP
THE ARVIDSSON LAUNCH ONCE MORE
AND SURGED DOWN THE GRAND CANAL.

TRUBCOCK LIMPED RAPIDLY PAST THE OFFICES OF THE BRITISH VICE CONSUL ON INTO SAN TROVASO. THE MANAGER OF THE LOCANDA MONTIN MET HIM AT THE RESTAURANT DOOR.

"YOU CALL ABOUT THE ENGLISH LADY?"

"YES", REPLIED TRUBCOCK. "WHERE IS SHE?"

"SHE CHECKED OUT TEN MINUTES AGO."

"WAS SHE CARRYING ANYTHING UNUSUAL?" ASKED THE DETECTIVE.

"ONLY A BLOCK OF WHAT I TOOK TO BE BILLIARD CHALK," REMARKED THE MANAGER, TAPPING HIS WRIST.

"SHOW ME HER ROOM!" ROARED TRUBCOCK.

"CERTAINLY, SIGNOR, FOLLOW ME!"

TRUBCOCK PUSHED OPEN THE DOOR TO ROOM 18. STEPPING OVER THE MOUND OF GREEN DUST THE TWO MEN CROSSED TO THE TABLE BY THE SHUTTERED WINDOW. THE MANAGER REACHED DOWN INTO THE SHADOWS.

"AN ENGLISH LADY'S LIPSTICK, I BELIEVE."

TRUBCOCK BIT HARD ON HIS LIP. THE
MANAGER TWISTED THE LIPSTICK SLOW-
LY CLOCKWISE, USING BOTH HANDS. A
SHINY METAL PANEL SLID OPEN JUST
ABOVE THE MONOGRAMMED BASE.
 A TRIANGLE OF GREEN PAPER CRASHED
TO THE FLOOR.

"WHAT IS IT?" ASKED THE MANAGER.

TRUBCOCK BENT DOWN AND PICKED IT UP.
HE READ ALOUD THE WORDS HE SAW:

PRESTON NORVELL
188B BROUWER SGRACHT
11.30 TUESDAY. NO SNOOD.

"WHAT IS IT?" REPEATED THE MANAGER.
"IT'S WORDS ON A PIECE OF PAPER," SNAPPED
TRUBCOCK. "BUT IT COULD STILL PROVE TO
BE IMPORTANT. CAN I USE YOUR PHONE?"

A CALL TO INTERPOL IN PARIS TOLD HIM
WHAT HE WANTED TO KNOW. THERE WAS NO
RACING AT CHANTILLY THAT DAY AND
NORVELL WAS A KNOWN RACKETEER
OPERATING FROM ONE OF THE SEEDIEST
AREAS OF AMSTERDAM.

TRUBCOCK PLACED A CALL TO HIS WIFE,
BACK IN ENGLAND.
"EDNA", HE GRUNTED, "CAN YOU HEAR ME?"
"OH, YES DEAR," SHE REPLIED, SLIPPING
A CHARRED OVEN GLOVE UNDER THE
COOKER. "WHEN ARE YOU COMING HOME?"
I THINK I'LL BE THERE SOONER THAN
I THOUGHT", HE SAID.
"OH, I CAN'T WAIT. WE'LL MOVE OUT INTO
THE COUNTRY, BUY A LITTLE COTTAGE
AND WHILE YOU'RE OUT PLAYING GOLF
I'LL COOK YOUR FAVOURITE DISHES FOR
YOU. I CAN SEE IT ALL NOW!"

"YES, DEAR. SO CAN I. BYE FOR NOW,"
SAID THE INSPECTOR AS HE SLOWLY
BUT FIRMLY REPLACED THE RECEIVER.

GLADYS SLIPPED OVER THE SWISS BORDER IN A STOLEN BUICK, SWITCHED CARS IN LUGANO AND SPED ON TO ZÜRICH. SHE STOPPED THERE OUTSIDE THE MASSIVE SPONGE FURNITURE DEPOSITORY ON ARVIDSSONSTRAT AND LOOKED FOR HER LIPSTICK. TWO HOURS LATER SHE OPENED THE THROTTLE OF THE BRIGHT YELLOW MONOPLANE, PULLED BACK THE JOYSTICK AND TOOK TO THE AIR. SHE CROSSED OVER INTO BELGIUM, INDISCRIMINATELY DESTROYING HABERDASHERY AND MEN'S OUTFITTING SHOPS IN LIÈGE, ANTWERP AND GHENT AS SHE WENT.

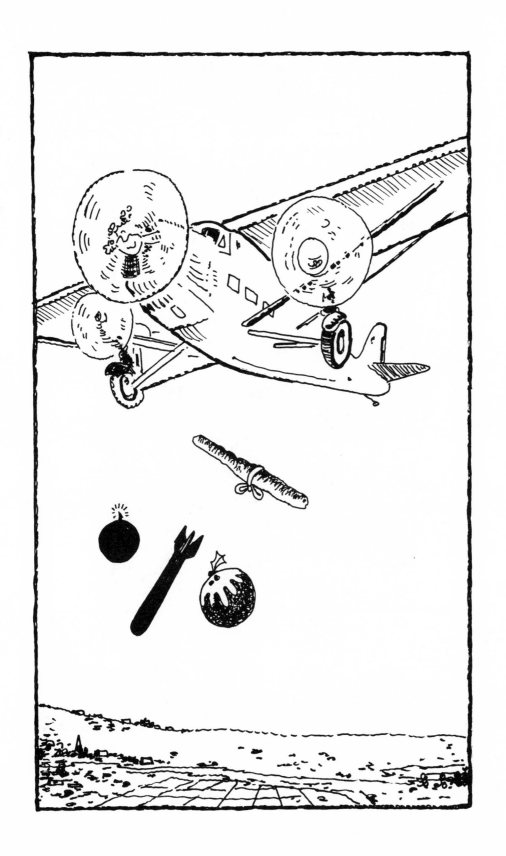

Chapter Twenty Six
TRUBCOCK'S TRIUMPH

Brouwersgracht, Amsterdam
Tuesday, 17ᵗʰ March 1957, 11.26 a.m.

A BARGE NOSED ALONG THE CANAL.
TRUBCOCK LOOKED AT HIS WRIST. HIS
WATCH WAS STILL THERE. HE CROSSED
THE ORANJEBRUG BRIDGE AND TURNED
RIGHT. A FIGURE DRESSED ALMOST
ENTIRELY IN BLACK EMERGED FROM THE
SHADOWS. THE DETECTIVE CALLED OUT,
"DON'T MAKE A MOVE, GLADYS
BABBINGTON MORTON. I'M DETECTIVE
INSPECTOR TRUBCOCK OF SCOTLAND
YARD AND YOU'RE UNDER ARREST!"

THE FIGURE TURNED SWIFTLY ROUND.
"HOW DID YOU KNOW?" HISSED GLADYS.

220

"I'M AFRAID YOU OVERLOOKED ONE SMALL
DETAIL, MISS MORTON."
GLADYS REMOVED THE BRIAR FROM HER
MOUTH, REPLACED IT WITH A CIGAR AND
GLARED AT HER CAPTOR.
"AND JUST WHAT WAS THAT?" SHE SNAPPED.
THE DETECTIVE POINTED TO HER FEET.

"MATCHING ARGYLLES. ALWAYS A DEAD
GIVEAWAY," HE NOTED AS HE SLIPPED THE
CUFFS OVER HER WRISTS.

IT ONLY REMAINED FOR THE DETECTIVE
INSPECTOR TO CLEAR HER EXTRADITION
PAPERS WITH THE DUTCH AUTHORITIES,

BEFORE BRINGING GLADYS BABBINGTON MORTON
BACK TO STAND TRIAL AT THE OLD BAILEY.

Chapter Twenty Seven
FINAL DETAILS

Wapping, London, 19th May 1957, 10.26 a.m.

AFTER TEN DAYS AT SEA, CAPTAIN "DICKY" SKIDMORE OF "HMS ENDEAVOUR", BEARING THE SPECIAL TASK FORCE, SLOWED DOWN THE ENGINES, BROUGHT HIS SHIP UP TWENTY FEET, CHECKED THE BEARINGS ON THE CHART AND RAISED PERISCOPE.

HE SIGHED DEEPLY. "I THINK WE MAY HAVE MADE A SLIGHT MISCALCULATION SOMEWHERE DOWN THE LINE", HE MUTTERED, TURNING TO FIX THE FIRST MATE WITH AN ICY GLARE.

DETECTIVE INSPECTOR TRUBCOCK RETURNED
IN TRIUMPH TO SCOTLAND YARD WHERE HE
WAS SUMMONED TO THE OFFICE OF CHIEF
SUPERINTENDENT "BULB REPLACEMENT"
GRIFFITH, A LEGEND WITHIN THE FORCE

AND ONE OF THE MOST BRILLIANT SHADOW
PUPPETEERS EVER TO COME OUT OF BIGGLES-
WADE. "AH, COME IN, TRUBWORTH. A BRILLIANT
JOB. SORRY TO HEAR ABOUT THE LEG!"

"IT'S MUCH BETTER NOW, SIR!"
"YOU'VE BEEN THROUGH DIFFICULT TIMES, TRUTTWORTH", NODDED THE SUPERINTENDENT.
"YES, WE NEARLY LOST HER IN VENICE, BUT THANKS TO CAPTAIN VAN KOOTEN OF ITALIAN SPECIAL OPERATIONS WE WERE ABLE TO SLIP TWO ENGINEERS INTO THE SUSPECT'S ROOM TO INSTALL THE VERY LATEST EAVESDROPPING EQUIPMENT. THEY WERE IN AND OUT INSIDE EIGHTEEN MINUTES. SHE NEVER KNEW HER ROOM WAS BUGGED," SMILED TRUBCOCK.
"SO THE OPERATION WAS SUCCESSFUL?"

"YES, THE INFORMATION PICKED UP IN
VENICE LED US DIRECTLY TO AMSTERDAM
AND THE INCRIMINATING ARGYLLES. THE
REST WAS ROUTINE," CONCLUDED TRUBCOCK.
"ABSOLUTELY WELL DONE, TRUTTLEY!"
ADDED HIS SUPERIOR.

"NOW ALL WE CAN DO IS TO
AWAIT THE VERDICT OF THE JURY.
IT'S BEEN ONE HELL OF A CASE
BUT YOU MANAGED TO PULL
THROUGH AND ENSURE THAT THE
WORDS 'SCOTLAND YARD' STILL
STRIKE TERROR INTO THE HEARTS
OF CRIMINALS ALL OVER THE WORLD.
I SUPPOSE YOU'LL BE DASHING
HOME NOW TO SEE MRS. TRUTTLE?"
"I THINK AFTER THE TRIAL, SIR,"
MUMBLED TRUBCOCK, SHIFTING
NERVOUSLY IN HIS CHAIR.

Chapter Twenty Eight
THE TRIAL

Central Criminal Court Nº 1
London E.C.1 , Wednesday
22nd May 1957 , 8.26 a.m.

SECURITY THE TRIAL OF GLADYS BABBINGTON MORTON BEGAN AT THE OLD BAILEY.

DETECTIVE INSPECTOR TRUBCOCK
FOUND HIMSELF FACING

THE FULL GLARE OF PUBLICITY
FROM THE WORLD'S PRESS

WHILST GLADYS WAS WHISKED

QUICKLY AND QUIETLY INTO NUMBER
ONE COURT VIA THE KITCHENS.

OVER THE NEXT TWO WEEKS A
PACKED COURTROOM HEARD THE
EVIDENCE OF TEACHERS, CHILD PSY-
CHOLOGISTS, AMERICANS, TWO EGYP-
TIANS, AND A REPRESENTATIVE FROM
THE NATIONAL SOCIETY FOR THE
GLOBAL PROMOTION OF BILLIARDS.

THE JURY WAS SHOWN TWO PHOTO-
GRAPHS OF THE EXACT SPOT WHERE
MᶜNALLY HAD DISAPPEARED AND A
PLASTER MODEL OF A CROSS-SECTION
OF CANNELLONI WAS PUT ON DISPLAY
NEXT TO EXHIBIT "A", A PULVERIZED
MOUND OF BILLIARD-TABLE PARTICLES.

ON THE EVENING OF 7th JULY 1957 THE
JURY RETIRED TO CONSIDER THEIR
VERDICT. IT WAS DELIVERED ON THE
MORNING OF THE 9th.

GUILTY ON ALL CHARGES.

JUDGE ALEXANDER DURNFIELD WOKE
UP WITH A START, THE MEMORY OF
EASTER IN BOULOGNE FADING SLOWLY
FROM HIS MIND. HE OPENED BOTH
EYES, TURNED TO FACE GLADYS AND
PRONOUNCED:

"OVER THE PAST TWO WEEKS THE
COURT HAS HEARD OF YOUR UTTER
CONTEMPT FOR RELATIVES, LOVERS,
AMERICANS AND BELGIANS.
  THIS, COUPLED WITH YOUR CALLOUS
DISREGARD FOR THE LAWS OF
CIVILIZED SOCIETY AND THE BASIC
TENETS OF TUSCAN CUISINE, HAVE
LED THE JURY TO REACH THEIR
VERDICT. DESPITE THE APPALLING
NATURE OF YOUR CRIMES, HOWEVER,
I HAVE DECIDED TO TAKE A LENIENT
VIEW, AND HEREBY SENTENCE YOU
TO A TERM OF LIFE IMPRISONMENT."

INSPECTOR TRUBCOCK RACED FROM THE PACKED COURTROOM TO THE NEAREST PUBLIC TELEPHONE. HE PUSHED THE COINS INTO THE SLOT AND DIALLED HOME. NOTHING HAPPENED. HE TRIED AGAIN, THEN SLAMMED DOWN THE RECEIVER AND PULLED OUT HIS NOTEPAD AND A PEN, AND BEGAN TO WRITE.

Dearest Edna, I can't believe it's all over! I'll be home before this letter arrives but I just had to write, all my love Gerald

HE RUSHED OUT OF THE KIOSK AND HAILED A TAXI.
"THE NEAREST POST OFFICE AND STEP ON IT, BUDDY!" HE CRIED AS THE BLACK CAB PULLED UP SHARPLY AT THE KERB.
"MY LUCKY DAY," GROANED THE GENIAL COCKNEY DRIVER, AS THEY PULLED OUT INTO THE TRAFFIC.

EDNA TRUBCOCK AWOKE AT 8 O'CLOCK AND SHUFFLED
DOWN THE CORRIDOR ON HER WAY TO SWITCH OFF THE
OVEN. THE MORNING PAPER CLATTERED THROUGH THE
LETTERBOX ON TO THE MAT.

SHE LOOKED DOWN, SCRATCHED HER NOSE
AND SHUFFLED ON INTO THE KITCHEN.

Chapter Twenty Nine
THE LAST STRAW

Netherwold Maximum Security
Prison, West Riding of Yorkshire
Wednesday 13th July 1957, 12.26 p.m.

GLADYS WAS DRIVEN THROUGH THE
PRISON GATES AT NETHERWOLD, THE
MOST NOTORIOUS NEW PURPOSE-BUILT
PRISON COMPLEX IN BRITAIN, WHOSE
CONTROVERSIAL POLICY OF SUBJECTING
ITS INMATES TO SIXTEEN HOURS A
DAY OF NON-STOP ENTERTAINMENT HAD
RECENTLY BEEN THE SUBJECT OF
DEBATE BY THE MEMBERS OF THE
HOUSE OF LORDS. SHE LOOKED UP AT THE
FLASHING NEON SIGNS PROCLAIMING:

AND PASSED ON THROUGH INTO THE
CENTRAL COURTYARD, WHERE GIANT
CUT-OUT FIGURES OF LAUGHING
POLICEMEN GREETED EACH NEWCOMER
TO NETHERWOLD.

HERE THE ARMOURED CAR STOPPED AND
GLADYS WAS LED ON FOOT UP A FAKE
ALPINE HILLSIDE PATH TO A GARISHLY LIT
GINGERBREAD COTTAGE, WHERE THE WARDEN
WAS WAITING TO MEET HER.

"WELCOME, MY DEAR! ALLOW ME TO
SHOW YOU THE FACILITIES HERE AT
NETHERWOLD. COME, FOLLOW ME..."

HE THREW OPEN A SMALL METAL DOOR.
GLADYS PEERED INSIDE.

"WE DON'T CALL THEM CELLS ANY MORE.
YOU'LL BE SLEEPING HERE. ENJOY YOUR STAY!"
BEAMED THE WARDEN.

THE CLOCK ON THE TRUBCOCK
MANTELPIECE CHIMED ELEVEN.
FOUR MINUTES LATER THE CUCKOO
CLOCK IN THE KITCHEN BUZZED
AND WHIRRED. AT TEN MINUTES PAST
ELEVEN, THE SMALL SPONGE BIRD
NOSED SLOWLY THROUGH THE MOCK
TYROLEAN DOORS DECORATED WITH
GARLANDS OF EDELWEISS AND
LODGED ITSELF THERE.
MRS. TRUBCOCK PICKED UP THE
LOCAL NEWSPAPER AND GLANCED
BRIEFLY AT THE FRONT PAGE BEFORE
TURNING SWIFTLY TO PAGE FIVE FOR
"RECIPE OF THE WEEK".

INSPECTOR TRUBCOCK ARRIVED AT
CHARING CROSS STATION, CAUGHT THE
10.26 TO GROATHAM, CHANGED AT
PAWSKLEY AND ARRIVED AT LOWER
BIDDLINGTON AT 5.28. HE SHUFFLED
THE LAST TWO MILES UP TO THE
HOUSE.

HE OPENED THE FRONT DOOR,
SNIFFED DEEPLY AND STEPPED INTO
THE HALLWAY, ANNOUNCING,
"I'M BACK, DEAR!"
"YOU'RE JUST IN TIME, MY DEAREST,"
REPLIED MRS. TRUBCOCK FROM THE
KITCHEN.
"I'VE A LITTLE SURPRISE FOR YOU!"
"AND WHAT MIGHT THAT BE, EDNA,
MY LOVE?"

"IT'S A NEW RECIPE, DEAR. I THINK
YOU'RE GOING TO FIND IT RATHER SPECIAL."